The Wolf

"You must take me for a fc   ....
tears betrayed him. He hated this as much as she did.

"No, not at all." She replied, "I might not even
change. Females don't change".

"We can't take that risk, you know that" he replied.
Howard stayed still. His finger rested on the trigger.
His hand held the slightest of tremors. "How could
you let him bite you?"

"Just kill her," ordered Natalie, "It's protocol".

Clara closed her eyes. "Just do it," Clara
whimpered. Tears fell down her face. A shot fired and
pain echoed through her. Her head thudded on the
ground. Darkness took over the bright sunny sky.

THE WOLF'S HUNTRESS

The Order Book One

Alessa Langley

ISBN 978-1-09876-099-1

Typeset in Times New Roman

Independently published by Sofia Vigo di Gallidoro

This book is dedicated to my amazing little girl, may you grow up strong and kind.

THE WOLF'S HUNTRESS

PROLOGUE

It had been one hell of a fight. Staring down at the body before her, Clara tried to get her breath back. Pain racked her body, yet her head stayed steady as she waited for any sign of life from the unnaturally large wolf. She lowered her gun as the fur receded on the wolf's body. Slowly the body morphed back into the six-foot-tall skinny form of the man she had lured into the woods. Brandon Cox was nothing more than a mutt with a record for stalking human women. Although he had never harmed anyone, he was a constant thorn in The Order's side, and she had been assigned to despatch him.

She hadn't quite understood why she had to do the job. He was nothing more than a runt. Any recruit could have taken the mission and be back for dinner, even those in training. It had been obvious to her during her observations that Brandon didn't take good care of himself. He still ate like a human, no extra calories to rebuild the energy he wasted by shifting. His body was skinny compared to other Lycans she had taken down. He didn't have much reserve energy to use if he got attacked. Which is why she was shocked that she was tired from fighting him. He had to have known that she was a hunter and he was her mark, otherwise all it would have taken was a swift shot to the head. Instead it had been a scrabble, as soon as she got deep enough into the woodland not to be seen by passers-by Brandon had jumped up into the trees using the canopy as a cover.

Sighing Clara slumped down on the ground. Her eyes fell to the man's chest. It wasn't moving, and there was no sound coming from him. He was dead. But he hadn't gone quietly as she expected. Clara assessed the scratches along her bare arms. The wolf had pinned her and knocked her gun away. If it hadn't been for her now-in-tatters leather jacket her wrists would have been slashed, and she would have bled out. Lowering her head, she took in her chest. Blood darkened her dark grey t-shirt along her right side. The fabric had torn ever so slightly. It looked nothing more than another scratch. Ignoring the wound Clara pulled her mobile from her pocket and speed-dialled the number. "Clara, where are you?" asked a friendly male voice that could only belong to James.

"I'm still in Ash Forest. Target has been dispatched. Is there anyone nearby to help?" Clara informed and asked. She could hear James tapping away trying to pinpoint her exact location within Ash Forest.

"I'm having trouble pinpointing your GPS, how far are you from your car?" he asked in monotone.

Clara looked around for any indication of where she was. The only thing she knew is that she hadn't walked that far into the woods. "I'm probably only a mile east of the car, in the forest" she replied guessing the details. Once again tapping echoed down the phone as James tried to narrow down the search. He hummed to himself for a moment.

"It seems, Howard took a recruit into Ash Forest just two hours before you started your mission," he mused, "I'll phone him and send them in your direction, just stay where you are". At that he hung up.

In the sudden silence, Clara shoved her phone in her pocket and went back to checking herself out. The wound on her right side wasn't hurting as much as the rest, but instead it itched as if she had rolled in nettles. Sighing she rolled up her t-shirt and looked down at the wound. Dread instantly filled her. It wasn't a scratch. She had been bitten. Thinking very slowly, Clara tried to think of what to do next. But the only thought that kept coming back to her is that other Hunters were their way to her. Quickly she zipped up her jacket hiding the blood-stained top. The only thought in her mind now was keeping her wounds hidden for as long as possible. Until she could get the body dumped and into her own car, she wasn't going to be safe. She knew The Order's procedures, not that she followed them to a 'T', but she knew the other hunters did. Of course, if she decided to run The Order would find her at some point. They always found their targets. But Clara's instincts always pushed her survive at any cost, even if there was a threat in the future.

Taking deep breathes Clara tried to get her mind to focus on a get-away plan. Just because she was bitten didn't mean she was going to become a Lycan, but The Order wouldn't take that risk. Instead they would kill her on the spot when they found out. If she could get away for a month, they would merely think she fell off the grid for a while. Within that month she would find out if she was going to change. If she did, then she would try to track down a Pack, and if she didn't, she would return to The Order. Seemed easy enough in her mind, but it was putting it into practice which was going to be the hard part.

"Clara?" called a voice from deeper in the forest. Howard Jones, the blonde Adonis was The Order's top Hunter and Clara's on-and-off lover.

"I'm over here," she called out in return. She didn't give any clues as to where she was, as he was extremely good at tracking. About five minutes later, he stood just a few metres away from her with his new prodigy, Natalie McKenzie, following behind him. As he reached Clara he looked down at the naked body of Brandon Cox. "I see, you've been busy" he stated with a smile. Clara smiled and stood up.

"I see you didn't get off unscathed," taunted Natalie. Her eyes instantly searched for weakness in Clara.

"I'm sure you would have come off worse, rookie," Clara said dryly. Her eyes instantly revealed her boredom of Natalie. The youngster had been trying to point out Clara's flaws ever since she entered The Order. Natalie was nothing more than a power grabber who believed she could gain prestige by winning Howard over.

"I thought we were meant to shoot from a distance," Natalie mentioned pointing out yet another failure of Clara's.

Clara merely glared at the girl as she stepped closer to Howard. On a job, Howard enforced the fact that they couldn't show any indication that they were in a relationship. Clara, however, was never one to follow rules, but she liked the distance as it helped her feel independent. Although, it didn't stop her wanting Howard to turn around, put the girl in her place and show some sort of affection towards herself. Instead he platonically eyed her up, "Are you okay?" he asked assessing her appearance.

"I'm fine, just a few scratches," she lied with a bright smile. Howard just nodded and took her word for it. Natalie, however, narrowed her eyes at Clara but stayed quiet.

Howard instantly began to take command. It didn't matter that it had been Clara's mission to dispatch the Lycan Mutt. All that mattered was that he was the commanding officer and therefore that put him in charge. "We need to make the body unidentifiable and then get rid of it" he stated looking down at the man. His face was already banged up from having the butt of her gun slammed in his face several times. But that wasn't enough. "Clara, get the legs. Natalie you need to look out for witnesses while we carry him to the car" he ordered as he moved to the Brandon's head.

They picked up the body and slowly made their way out of the forest. Sunlight hit them as they stepped out on to the country road. Clara's black

Land Rover looked inviting enough for her to run to, if she hadn't been with Howard and Natalie. Several times on the walk Natalie had spied Clara favouring one side and now they had dumped the body in Howard's car, she wasn't about to let it go.

"Did he get you on your right?" Natalie asked sounding sincere, although her eyes betrayed her.

"Clara?" Howard turned around and took in how Clara was standing, "Are you sure you are okay?"

"I'm fine, I told you" she replied with a fake warm smile. She wasn't fine. The bite was starting to burn, and the itchiness was unbearable.

"We're meant to assess all wounds before heading back to Headquarters," Natalie spoke up. Her eyes narrowed on Clara.

Swallowing hard, Clara stared up at Howard. She mentally prayed he wouldn't ask her to show him the wound. It was a mere bite. She was fine. She wasn't bleeding enough to gain medical attention. She had helped carry the body back to the car, that alone showed it hadn't gone too deep. Howard shouldn't be suspicious. "Okay," Howard said, rubbing his forehead as if he had dealt with corrections from Natalie all day, "Clara take off your jacket so I can see your wounds".

Clara complied with huff knowing her t-shirt hid the worst one. Howard pulled her arms out and looked at the scratches running along them. They were still bleeding slightly but they weren't overly deep, due to her jacket acting like a buffer. "They just need disinfecting and a bit of wrapping, nothing to go see the medical officers about," Clara commented pulling her arms away. He let her arms fall and then his eyes landed on her top.

"Did he get you there?" he asked.

"No, it's merely damage when he got my arms," she replied lying again. Natalie tapped her foot and looking impatient about what she had enforced.

"I need to check, anyway" sighed Howard, who had been more forceful about checking wounds before he had gotten to know Clara. Before he had met her

Howard had followed every rule in the book, but Clara had shown him how to bend the rules. Now it seemed he was as tired of them as she was.

"Why don't we check when we get back to our place?" she smiled stepping closer to him. She rested her hands against his chest and smiled up at him. "I have three days off now, so we can relax. I'm merely scratched" she smiled as she leaned into him.

"Clara?" his voice was laced with surprise and suspicion, "Just let me see" he pushed.

"Why?" she argued back. Her mind instantly reprimanded her. If she kept playing along with the flirtatious girlfriend, Howard would have given in. Yet, when pushed she always came out on the defensive. Her instincts seemed to always let her down.

"Let me see" he ordered; his voice become darker as he glared down at her. He knew something was up.

Clara took a few steps back and eyed both. In training she was faster than most. She wasn't stronger but she could fight better than the majority of the hunters in The Order. The only one who surpassed her was Howard, who had been her mentor before becoming her lover. She could run and hide in the forest, but he would find her. She settled on a hope; the hope that he loved her enough to make her the exception to the most enforced rule in The Order. The bitten must die.

Her hands trembled as she lifted her top. In a split second everything changed. Howard's eyes turned cold. Clara watched in disbelief as Howard pulled his gun out and aimed it right her head. "Howard?" she whispered. Her heart lurched and her stomach dropped. She was going to die, and by the hands of someone she thought loved her, or at least cared for her deeply. "Howard, please" she whimpered. Her lips trembled as she slowly knelt on the ground.

"You must take me for a fool, Clara" he said. His tears betrayed him. He hated this as much as she did.

"No, not at all." She replied, "I might not even change. Females don't change".

"We can't take that risk, you know that" he replied. Howard stayed still. His finger rested on the trigger. His hand held the slightest of tremors. "How could you let him bite you?"

"Just kill her," ordered Natalie, "It's protocol".

Clara closed her eyes. "Just do it," Clara whimpered. Tears fell down her face. A shot fired and pain echoed through her. Her head thudded on the ground. Darkness took over the bright sunny sky.

CHAPTER 1

Caleb Daevers watched as Peter, the only doctor he trusted, work away at the woman he had found. It was completely unlike him to help any outsiders, but this one was different. Not only was she a slim attractive blonde, but she also had the scent of a Lycanthrope about her. A quality in a woman that had been non-existent for fifty years. However, if she was treated properly and proved that she was a full Lycan, she would be the key to regaining the female half of their race.

The sound of metal upon metal rang through the room as Peter dropped another bullet into his surgery tray.

"She was shot with a silver bullet," said Peter, pointing to the bullet he just pulled out, "She was in one hell of a fight before being shot though. There are scratches covering her arms which have already started to heal." He pointed out each wound. It wasn't long before he lifted the ripped hem of her t-shirt to reveal the bite that had sped up the healing process. "She was bitten before being shot, there's a small allergic reaction around the bullet which show the toxins in the bite had already started to take effect," stated Peter.

"Is there anything else?" Caleb asked, having only really noticed the full extent of her injuries.

"She has a tattoo similar to The Order's branding on her forearm," he stated turning the woman's wrist round to show a sequence of numbers tattooed vertically along it, 4673829. Caleb memorised the numbers and then looked back up at the woman's face. She had barely been breathing when he had found her. The silver had been killing her slowly where the bullet alone hadn't.

"Get a picture of her when you've bandaged her up. I need to see if anyone recognises her," Caleb said before leaving the room.

Hurriedly he jogged up the stairs to the ground floor and headed to his study. The number on the woman's forearm needed to be researched. He walked in and sat down at his desk. He booted up his computer and instantly started trying to gain access to The Order's database. The database was becoming increasingly hackable into nowadays since they were continually updating their records, sometimes leaving the files open to public access. He typed in the number into the search and suddenly the woman's face popped up on the screen. Agent Clara Richards, Deceased.

He opened the file and read though the data. According to the file, she was twenty-four years old, with six years of experience after training working as a Hunter in The Order. The file didn't state what had happened in the most recent mission, only listed her abilities and personal information. Quickly he copied the data and worked about blocking The Order from tracking his usage. Once off their network, he printed off the information then just sat staring up at the ceiling as he wondered about the woman downstairs.

His mind tried to get around the fact he had brought an outsider to Pack Territory and the fact he didn't feel the urge to attack her for the fact she was a hunter. The mere fact should have thrown him into a rage, but he couldn't bring himself to leave the female for death to take her. He knew he had brought trouble into his den, but he wasn't completely sure it came in the form of the women he had saved.

As he put his head in his hands, Michael walked into his study. "I didn't think you were the type to go saving damsels in distress," he joked leaning about the doorframe with his arms crossed over his chest.

"She was bitten, I had no other option," Caleb answered back as he looked up at Michael.

"Well, there had to be something special about her to gain your attention," Michael joked walking into the room and perching on the arm of the sofa by Caleb's chair. "So, who is she?" he asked.

"Clara Richards," Caleb said handing Michael the file he had printed off. Michael carefully took in the details, his jaw tensing repeatedly.

"A hunter turned Lycan?" he mused to himself. After a few minutes his head lifted, "Don't they kill their own when they get bitten?"

"Peter found a silver bullet in her chest," Caleb mentioned.

"Shit," was the only thing Michael could say. Caleb had saved a hunter that had been shot by The Order. Plus, that said hunter could be a female Lycan.

After a few minutes of silence Michael looked towards the doorway. "The only question left is to find out what happened on her last mission I guess," said Michael. He paused for a moment before adding, "and whether she wants to stay a Lycan".

"Get a few people together and get them to scan Ash Forest for any clues," ordered Caleb.

"Ash Forest?"

"That's where I found her, shoved into a thicket" Caleb practically spat. He was shocked at the fact The Order would treat their own so poorly.

"Maybe you should stay down there with her, in case she wakes up confused and frightened," Michael suggested with a shrug before leaving to round up a search party. Once he had left, Caleb went back to delving into his own thoughts. He leaned back in his chair, but this time closed his eyes.

After an hour of sitting down added with spurts of pacing his study, Caleb headed back to the basement. Down the hidden staircase he walked into a well-lit room that had been the foundations of the house. On one side he had walls filled with files on every Mutt and Pack Lycan in the region, as well as Agents and Hunters they had come across. Round to the right of the staircase hidden directly from view was a silver lined room, the cage. The cage itself was big enough to comfortably sit eight people, and definitely strong enough to withstand the strength of a Lycan in the pits of feral rage. Directly in front of him, as few steps ahead, stood a pair of thick double doors that led to where the Huntress Clara Richards was lying unconscious. The medical room.

The medical room was not a high-tech makeshift lab, but nor was it a hovel. Peter Louvell had kept it clean and hygienic. He had set it up with minimal equipment, but enough to help several pack members at once if needs be. He had made sure that there were three metal frame beds inside the room. The rest of the room was bare apart from the wall to the left to the door, which was lined with wall cabinets and counter tops, where Peter kept his medical supplies.

Caleb entered and the irritating smell of chemicals hit his sensitive nose. Wrinkling his nose slightly, he stared over at Peter who was sitting at his desk with his head in his hands whilst a petit white-haired woman whispered to him. Caleb's back instantly straightened as he noticed Mary Kael. Mary turned her glare on to him and stormed over. "How can you keep her down here?" she bellowed up at him.

"I believe that that is my business, and you know you shouldn't be down here," Caleb stated back trying to use the power that came with his Alpha status. Unfortunately for him, although Mary was human, she had brought him up since he was three. To her, he was nothing more than a child who needed to be reprimanded most of the time. Mary crossed her arms and tapped her foot. At five-foot-three, she had nothing in her height to intimidate the men of the Pack who all stood over six-foot, but as soon as her foot tapped, they bent to her will. Swallowing hard Caleb looked over at Peter, "Has she shown any signs of waking up?" he asked.

"The wounds have all but healed, but other than that there is no different in her pulse," Peter said standing up. Mary audibly tutted in response to her question being ignored. "I'll give her a few more hours, before I check on her again later" Peter added before heading towards the door.

"All that girl needs is a decent sleep, and she would get that in a bed upstairs," Mary added glaring at both men.

"She stays down here until she wakes," Caleb pushed looking back at Mary.

"Oh no, she doesn't. A human girl cannot stay down here. She needs hospital care," Mary stated.

"She isn't human, Mary" Caleb stated back, "She's one of us".

Mary's eyes widened as she looked back at the girl. The blonde haired, pale girl that looked all too small and weak to be anything other than human. Mary looked the woman over once more. She took in the bandages covering both arms, the bruises covering the woman's face, and the patch on the right side of her stomach. The t-shirt had been pulled up enough to reveal an array of scars along her stomach. "She's…." Mary stumbled over the idea, "But I was told you were all male".

"Until fifty years ago they were just as common," Caleb mused. He hadn't added why or how, because it didn't matter now. Not now there was a key to bringing females back. Mary merely stared at him. No one had informed her of their history, she had just accepted them without explanation. "Oh, okay," she said before looking back at Caleb. Her eyes stayed on his face for a moment. A mother's worried glance. "I'm going to see what Edmund is getting up to in the garden," she excused herself.

Caleb sat down by the woman's bed, watching for indication of life. Her breathing was steady but slow. Her heart beat never quickened to show she was waking up. Her body lay still.

Hours passed and he was still sitting in the chair, his eyes focused on the bite. His mind wondered over how it could be possible for her to accept the Bite. His father had proved human women couldn't survive getting the bite. Jeffery Daevers, the last Alpha, had spent all of his free time hunting down women he believed held the key to bringing females back into the Lycan race. Everyone turned a blind eye to what their Alpha was doing, never really looking for evidence against him. That was, until Jeffery had finally taken an interest in his son.

After Caleb had shown Alpha-like abilities, Jeffery had seen fit to take his son under his wing. He had taught Caleb to lead, to hunt and finally to continue his work; to bring the females back into existence. It had taken Caleb witnessing one woman suffering through the poison of the bite to overthrow his father. He had only been twenty-one at the time, but it had been needed. Once he was Alpha, he found out it had been more than just a handful of women that had died from his father's bite. The number had almost reached triple figures by the time he had stopped his father's experiment. No woman had ever shown signs of even possibly surviving the bite.

Now before him lay a woman that wasn't writhing in agony, spitting up blood and pleading for mercy. Instead she was merely unconscious from silver poisoning and was gaining a stronger Lycan scent with every second. Caleb scratched the back of his neck confused by her very existence. How the hell was she even possible? He thought to himself. She should have been dead before Peter had even finished fishing out the bullet.

The door opened and Caleb's head shot round to see Michael. "Anything?" he asked as he watched his Beta step further into the room. Michael stared at the woman, Clara.

"She looks more like a Chihuahua with a sore paw than a vicious Lycan," joked Michael before turning to Caleb to deliver his findings. "It would seem no one has ever met her, but there are rumours of an Agent Richards. It would seem missy here preferred not to follow The Order's rules when it came to hunting," he said with a proud smile. Michael had never been impressed by humans using guns from a distance. In his mind there was no courage in their method. "It would also seem many Mutts are more scared of her than they are of us," he added, "I think we've found our deterrent".

"That is if she accepts the fact she can't go back," Caleb stated, "You never know, she may cling to the human side and try to return to The Order."

"Then we'll just have to convince her otherwise," Michael replied looking back down at the woman. "Mary is ranting and raving upstairs about how you should be giving the girl a bed upstairs."

"Once she wakes up and answers our questions, she'll get the spare bed". They both knew Clara Richards was staying whether she wanted to or not. Until she was awake, they had no idea where she would sleep out of the two options. Those options were either a well-furnished bedroom all to herself to do with what she liked, or the cage until she accepted her fate.

By six o'clock in the evening Clara still had not shown any signs of waking up. Caleb stood up from his chair. His eyes lingered on her face. Her skin was paler than when he had brought her into the house. But her eyes flickered back and forth beneath her lids. Her mind must have been running wild whilst her body lay still. Caleb turned away from her and headed for the door. It was time he socialised with everyone else instead of babysitting an unconscious woman, at least for a couple of hours.

"Howard...." her voice croaked. Caleb turned instantly; his eyes wide with shock. "No...." she croaked again. Her voice was raw, and her lips trembled. The words were weak as they passed her mouth. Tears fell from her closed eyes. Her heartbeat, however, stayed the same steady pace. Caleb breathed in trying to work his mind around what had happened. Her breathing slowed. A small sigh passed her lips before he watched her roll onto her side. He was relieved to see that Clara was no longer unconscious due to her wounds, she just needed a little more rest.

"Mary?" Caleb called out as soon as he returned to the ground floor of his house. He wandered towards the kitchen where food was brewing. "I need your help for once," he added with a smile. The kitchen door flew open to reveal Mary. Her white hair was pulled back away from her face, which had a speck of flour on the right cheek.

"You sure do pick your timing," she stated trying to seem cross, although her eyes were lit up with the fact her surrogate son needed her. "What is it anyway?" she asked crossing her arms.

"I was going to ask you to listen out for the girl while I rest up," Caleb stated as he mimicked her body language, "But I guess I could ask Leonard"

"You would ask Leonard?" Mary's eyes bulged, "He wouldn't even know whether she was alive or dead. Just leave the door open, I'll listen out for her". She said waving her spoon at him. Caleb kissed her on the forehead before walking into his study.

As he stepped inside, Caleb knew he wasn't alone. Michael and Edmund sat on the small sofa waiting for him. In that moment he knew that they had found out something more from the pack's all-day search of Ash Forest. Slowly he sat down in his office chair, turned to them and waited for them to speak. They looked at one another as if deciding who would speak first. After a short moment Michael spoke up, "We found the sight of conflict between the woman and a stray Mutt," he stated, "Joseph identified the Mutt as Brandon Cox. From our records, he has been laying low for the past few months and no reason why he would be a target of The Order".

"We'll have to ask her if she knows why," Caleb mused, keeping that question in mind.

"There was also a smell of death in that area," added Edmund, "No matter how the fight played out, the Mutt died from the hand of the Hunter downstairs." His voice became darker. The hatred he felt for The Order was evidently forming his opinion on what had taken place.

"There were shells on the floor, all had silver traces," Michael said sticking to facts, "The Mutt was probably killed there and then moved towards the road, which a trail of blood and mixed scent suggests."

"There was no evidence of anyone else being there, but she couldn't have shot herself, could she?" mused Michael.

Silence hit the stilled room. None of the men looked at each other as they wondered about how the woman had gotten injured. Had she shot herself? No one in the Pack truly knew how to investigate a murder scene, only to investigate scents and to track people. It was how they worked. If a stray went missing, they either showed up after a few months or they didn't. There was no need to investigate unless masses were disappearing. But this Hunter was different, her circumstances were different.

CHAPTER 2

A small spot of pain ached in the right side of her head. She had been lying down too long. Her eyes slowly opened. Bright light blinded her for a moment, causing her to blink rapidly against it. As she became accustomed to the light, she looked around her. The room was white-walled with cabinets lining the far wall to her right and two more beds lay out along the wall to her left. Clara knew that she was not back at Headquarters just by the size of the room. The medical facility at Headquarter would be noisy with nurses and doctors patrolling the gangway in the middle of the two rows of beds, there would be beeping from machines and chatter from patients. Clara moved slowly, her hands bracing her as she sat up. Material fell to her hip calling her attention to look downwards at herself.

Her eyes clung to the bandages on her arms. The t-shirt she had been wearing just the other day was caught on a large gauze patch on her abdomen. Moving slowly, she let her fingers graze the top of the dressing as she pulled her top up further. Bruising marred her normally tanned torso. Small patches of red stained the gauze. Clara slowly removed the bandage to reveal what had stayed a hidden memory.

There, on her side, lay the horror that would change her life. Clara swallowed hard on the reality. Her mind filled with images from her last hunt. She couldn't remember exactly when she had been bitten, only that she must have been bitten whilst she was tackled by the Mutt. Then the final terrible image hit. Howard standing before her with the gun aimed directly at her. Her heart stilled; her breathing became erratic. Her eyes looked wildly around the room, as if he would step out of a corner and try again.

Out of fear she moved and propelled herself off the bed. Once her bare feet were on the ground she looked around for any evidence of where she was. A newspaper or a calendar, but there was nothing.

She ripped the bandages from her forearms revealing cuts that stared back at her. They were almost healed; she had to have been unconscious for weeks. Her mind struggled to regain logical thinking. She no longer focused on what was around her but instead she tried to piece things together in her mind. Had Howard shot her or did something else happen? Her body shook with the panic. Her hands roamed her body trying to find evidence that she had been shot.

Sure enough her fingers found something. She lowered the collar of her once grey top and looked down at a wound in the centre of her chest. It had healed to the point it was no more than scabbing with a blue ring circled it. It was a colouration she was used to. On Lycans it meant a reaction to silver. She slowed her breathing, trying to calm herself. Her hand stayed on the small mark. He had shot her. Anger filled her.

Not caring that she was dressed in a blood-stained ripped t-shirt and matching almost completely destroyed jeans she stormed out of the room she had found herself in. Her eyes ignored the glow to her right as she exited the room and instead she found the nearest exit. A stairway leading towards a door that had been left half open.

She flew up them and through the half-opened door. Her mind focused on one thing. Revenge. How could someone shoot their partner for four years in the chest, over one little bite? Did she mean absolutely nothing to him? As she found herself standing and fuming in a hallway, her eyes darted in search of a door that would lead to freedom. There, she had found it. Half running, she charged to the front door and pushed through.

Warm air hit her. Sun blazed down and called her outside. The calm breeze and sunshine did nothing to calm her anger, but it did cause her to halt. Something was watching her. Fear bit into her. Her feet itched to run, to do something yet she stayed frozen watching the outside world. Something told her to stay in the building she was in, but she told herself she wasn't safe. Nowhere was safe until she got revenge. Gritting her teeth, she sprinted from the door into the outside world. "No, you can't go out there!" screamed a woman's voice behind her. Clara didn't care, she just ran.

She stayed on a set path before she felt something behind her. As trained, she took to the treeline beside the path. Clara darted from shadow to shadow. Her blue eyes focused on what was directly in front of her. The ground was rough on her bare feet, but it was nothing to pain that racked her mind.

Clara picked up pace, ignoring what her senses were telling her. Sounds filled the air as if warning her she had gone too far, but she kept running. Anger fuelled her running, yet the slow ache of her wounds kept reminding her to slow down.

The sounds around her slowly became clearer. Voices echoed from beyond her eye line. "I knew the packs were hiding them," said a voice to her right. Clara stopped and took in her surroundings. She had run too far into the woodland. There was no path running alongside her now, and there were no clear markings telling her where she now stood.

"Just wait, a little bit further and she is out of their territory," whispered another. Clara darted round, her eyes searching for the owners to the voices.

"Why wait?" hissed a clear booming voice. Clara turned quickly to look behind her. "The pack wolves are probably still in their safe little house" it added with a cruel hiss.

As her eyes focused on a shadow beyond the trees, she watched as it moved. It stalked her movements and watched her in return. Light flickered through the leaves lighting small areas around her. She gasped for air as she realised she was surrounded. Men watched her from afar. She had to run. Run to safety.

Instinctively she raced back the way she came. She wildly watched the area behind her from time to time. Her anger had faded into blinding fear. She had no idea where she was or what she was dealing with. Clara was completely out of her depth. She scrambled through the woodland trying to return to the path.

A heavy force pushed her off course. Her left side slammed into the rough side of a tree. She winced and attacked the weight that held her. Hands gripped her wrists and held them down. Her eyes blazed with fear. "Get the fuck off me!" she yelled as she tried to get free. Every manoeuvre she used was counteracted, keeping her locked against the tree.

"I wouldn't move too much if I were you, those wounds you have were still pretty bad last time someone checked," he said moving his arms as if to pick her up. As soon as his hands moved from hers, she lashed out and shoved the person away.

"Don't touch me," she snarled at him. The man merely glared at her for a moment. His dark eyes watched her closely. Clara stayed where she was, her eyes locked on his.

"It's me or them," he added after a moment. Clara stared back at the way she had come. A group of men stood in the distance. No, not all men. Wolves stood amongst them. She had been stalked by a group of Lycans. Her stomach twisted as she turned back to the man who stood opposite her.

The man moved closer to her. His eyes filled with concern rather than those predatory ones watching her from the shadows. Her mind whirled with suspicions. Lycans were known to be tricksters; they could con a man into giving up life if they were inclined to. Her eyes narrowed on him as he approached. His hand moved to her elbow and pulled her away as if to help her walk.

"I'll be fine on my own," Clara snapped as she pulled her arm away. She quickened her pace as she walked back to the large house she had run away from.

"So that's the thanks I get for saving you," mumbled the man. Clara glared at him over her shoulder as he trudged behind her. "Saving you twice in fact" he added.

Clara stopped. She turned around and stared at the man. Over six-foot-tall he towered over her, but then all Lycans had height and strength on their side. Only a few had looks that let them blend in with the world, but the one before her was clean shaven and well-dressed unlike many she had met. "What did you mean by twice?" she questioned.

"I would say getting you medical attention after being shot counted as saving you," he said calmly.

"You got me medical attention?" she asked with a raised brow and her arms crossed. Her logical mind told her to run, to stop interacting with him and just run like a bat out of hell. But she had never been one to truly pay attention to the logical and rule-abiding side to her brain.

"Do you even know what would happen, what trouble I could bring?" she asked in mocked anger. Her eyes watched his reaction, each movement measured in her head about what he was thinking. His lips twitched as if he wanted to smile. Then his eyes changed from dark amber to a blazing gold.

"I know exactly what you'll become" he said not even trying to hide his pleasure at the thought of a female in his pack.

"Just great," she mumbled to herself as she turned back round to continue walking.

She must have been out of her mind to return to the house, but there was something about it that made her feel safe. It was only her mind that made her falter. She couldn't. No, she wouldn't trust anyone. The only person she would trust was herself, and whatever she had been made into, to help her live along enough to get the answers she had been searching for her whole life.

As her feet hit the rough ground of the driveway she looked up at the house. It was purely made up of aging red brick with small additions added on each side. Ivy wound around the front door and up towards the top left window. Moss had worked its way into the cracks in the dark slate roof. The house itself was small against the crowding woodland around it, yet it was a picture-perfect place for Lycans to settle down in.

As she stepped inside the house, she was greeted by an aging woman glaring at the man that now stood behind Clara. "Caleb, I cannot believe you would let her go running around in her condition," the woman criticized, "she has been unconscious for almost 24 hours, and you let her outside. Honestly, I have to do everything around here" she yelled. Her eyes landed on Clara and suddenly Clara felt the need to back away. "You must be starving, come on in and I'll get you something to eat".

Clara was hustled further into the hallway by the woman until the man behind her shut the front door, and locking her in. "I bet Caleb has even failed to introduce himself and most definitely has yet to introduce the rest of us," the woman moaned glaring over her shoulder at the tall dark-haired man. The woman smiled and put her hand to her chest in an elegant fashion, "I am Mary Kael, and I am as close to a mother all the riff-raff here have". By the way her glare turned into a motherly gaze proved her point. Clara bit her lip; she had never seen anyone as her mother since the accident.

"I guess I should make the introductions then," said the dark-haired man, that Mary had called Caleb. "I am Caleb Daevers, the pack Alpha". With just the word, he had straightened and pulled himself up to his full height. Even so Clara could not find him intimidating. He was too young, although older than herself, and seem too kind in appearance to be classed as intimidating. "The usual lot you'll find lurking around my house are just through the door to your left," he said motioning her to move.

Clara slowly sidestepped and peered round the doorframe. There sat three men, all with their eyes set on her. Only one set her on edge. He sat in the centre of the sofa, with a slightly aging face. His body was still well built, showing he was still active, whist his eyes narrowed cruelly. His hair and eyes matched with a cold grey colour that stood out against his lightly tanned skin. Her gut twisted. Childhood memories flooded her mind.

"To the left we have Leonard," Caleb introduced.

"Call me Leo," he smiled subtly. Clara took in his startling appearance. His eyes were an outstanding pale blue, which shone out from his dark complexion. Leo took up a large proportion of one sofa, and Clara was pretty convinced he could very easily use just his size to intimidate challengers.

"In the middle we have Edmund," Caleb added moving along. Clara swallowed hard as she looked upon the man. He looked too much like an old foster parent of hers to the point she knew instantly that she wanted to avoid being in his company as much as possible. Edmund stood and strode towards her. His whole posture turned her back into that small twelve-year-old girl who hid away from her foster father. Her body shook uncontrollably, a part of her wanted to run from the threat and the other wanted to attack. Her hands clenched and unclenched.

"This is the hunter?" Edmund asked Caleb as he just pointed at her, ignoring the fact she could hear him. He turned to Clara and looked her over, calculating her reaction to him. "I thought she would be more impressive than this," he scoffed before pushing past her.

Anger fuelled her from somewhere deep inside. Throughout her childhood, men had looked at her and sneered. They liked her appearance, blue-eyed and blonde-haired child but as soon as they heard of her personality or her hobbies, they turned away from her. They never liked her for long. After a matter of weeks, sometimes months, she would be sent back because the men didn't like her as she wouldn't fit into their perfect little world. This time she was older. She was no longer vulnerable and defenceless.

Clara's hand shot her. Her hand cuffed his throat whilst a growl emitted from her throat. She could feel her eyes burning but she did not care. All she knew is that something inside her wanted to remind the man, Edmund, of his place, and that was several ranks below than her. Edmund turned slowly towards her. He snarled at her with glowing golden eyes. The growl he gave in return was to warn her off, to make her rethink her actions. But Clara didn't rethink, she couldn't think. She was listening to new instincts now. Ones that she knew would help her survive and keep her alive.

His hand moved to removed hers from his neck, but Clara swiped it away and threw him across the room. The other two men moved in front of him, blocking her view of him. A low steady hum, that had merely been an annoyance to Clara's ears since she held Edmund's throat, was now roaring. She became aware of a darkening shadow to her left. Her head tilted to see Caleb's eyes glowing gold and realised the roaring hum was coming from him. Her human instincts told her to run, but instead she turned and faced him head on. Her eyes landed on his and stayed there in a staring contest. The growling became louder, as a growl slowly grew from her.

After a few minutes of trying to stare Caleb down, Clara lowered her eyes and tilted her head, revealing her neck. Her brain knew what the move was, and she hated it. She was being submissive. It was like admitting she had done wrong. In her mind she had done nothing wrong, her brain kept telling her to put Edmund in his place and teach him to respect her. Shaking her head Clara returned to glaring at Caleb before turning back to the men that kept a defensive stance against her. "And you are?" she said roughly, crossing her arms and looking towards the blonde giant next to Leonard.

The giant gave her a smug smile in return. His eyes took her in with pure kindness, no hatred or judgement which she thought would be there. Instead he stepped forwards and held out his hand like any polite and civil human being. "Michael. Michael Faulkner" he said introducing himself, "Caleb's right hand man".

"Nice to meet someone who is polite for a change," Clara stated taking his hand and shaking it. His hand gripped hers tightly, to the point that when she tried to pull her hand free she stayed locked in the hand shake. He lowered his head, his eyes locked on hers before sniffing her wrist. Slightly confused and intrigued Clara kept her mouth shut and her fists to herself, for once. He straightened and smiled, "Welcome…"

"Why she is out of bed?" exclaimed a voice from the hall. As Clara turned, she noticed all of the men winced as they faced the person in the hall.

Clara stared at a thin man, with thick glasses and scruffy hair. His jacket was well-worn, and his shirt was creased, pointing out it was very possibly that he had fallen asleep whilst wearing it. His lips were pulled in a tight scowl. "She was injured only 24 hours ago, at the very least, and you have her up and about," he almost yelled, "She is meant to be resting…"

"She has a name," Clara mumbled before she could stop herself. The man glared in her direction as if he had heard her.

"Well, Hunter Clare Richards I believe you need to be downstairs in the medical room to be check over so I can make sure you are fit enough to be walking around," he snapped back.

"Peter, she just woke up. We're merely doing introductions, nothing too strenuous" Michael smiled with a shrug.

"Go downstairs with Peter," Caleb said as he placed a hand behind Clara's back urging her out of the room and into the hallway. "We need to make sure you didn't cause more damage with that little run of yours".

"Little run?!" Peter was becoming increasingly red in the face, "You let her run?"

"She snuck past us," Michael shrugged again.

A few more comments, and Peter looked closed to exploding. Although Clara found their interaction intriguing and was already trying to work out who truly had the power in their Pack, she felt it best to put Peter out of his misery. So, she smiled and calmly walked back towards the basement door. She climbed back down the stairs and just stopped at the bottom. Her eyes landed on the huge area just filled with files on bookcases, books on small desks and paper scattered along tables to the left of the medical room. They must have files on every creature that ever lived with the amount of information she saw. It was no wonder The Order found it hard to gain information on packs if the packs had it all on paper rather than on computers. Peter pushed her slightly with a moan, causing her to grumble in return but continued onwards into the medical room.

Once there, Peter instructed her to sit on the bed where she had been lying. Clara stared at the thin sheets, there was minimal blood spotting which seemed the wrong amount for someone who was shot and left to bleed out. In silence she sat down and just watched as Peter prepared bandages and put on gloves. "Can you take your top off please, use it to cover your chest if you wish" he said turning to her. His expression was like stone, he had become truly professional. Clara never got used to people who could hide all their emotions and thoughts, it seemed wrong. Sure, she had played the game before but she never had a completely different persona. She always kept a hint of human emotion in her being.

Clara took off her top and held it, so it covered her breasts but not the puckering bullet wound that rested just under her left collar bone. Peter stepped closer and with a gloved hand he tested the blue-tinted flesh around the bullet wound. To touch, the flesh was almost completely healed with no visual scarring except for the blue ring yet to look at it was clear to Peter that the flesh that lay deeper was not healing. The muscle that had been around the bullet when he pulled it out had been badly burnt, it wouldn't be surprising if it didn't heal completely.

Moving away from the wound, without any comment of what he thought best to do, he moved to her bandaged bite mark just above her right hip.

Quickly he pulled the bandaging off, causing Clara to wince. He carefully took in the appearance of the puncture marks. They weren't deep anymore. When Caleb had first brought her in, the right-hand side looked as if it had been close to being torn out. Yet, now it was almost as if she had been nipped by a frustrated puppy with a wide set jaw. It was still weeping although it wasn't as bad as it was for other bitten Mutts, which was surprising as they usually had the same healing rate. Leaning back, he slowly removed the bandaging from both her arms and looked at the closing wounds. Within a day or so her arms would return to normal with no sign of the claw marks. Peter moved and sat down in his chair.

"Can I put my top back on now?" Clara asked cutting his introspective thoughts short.

"Oh, sure," he replied pushing his glasses up his nose. "Caleb" he called barely shouting the name. Clara quickly slipped on her top carefully around the bite.

The door to the medical room opened and Caleb walked in. He ignored Clara, who stayed perched on the cot bed, and headed towards Peter. "You called?" he asked.

"I think you need to know," Peter paused and looked towards Clara, "She is healing at the rate of a pure-born, rather than at the rate of a bitten stray"

"There's a difference in healing speeds?" queried Clara, who was completely unconvinced. Caleb, however, glared at her and stormed over.

"Show me your wounds" he ordered with a dark expression on his face.

"No," She bit back as she stilled that small voice in the back of her mind that told her to follow his orders.

"Show me your wounds now" Caleb ordered again, this time an overwhelming pressure filled the room. Peter seemed to cower and pull himself further back in his chair whilst Clara stayed firm glaring up at Caleb.

Once again, they entered an intense staring contest, but this time it fell short when Caleb gripped Clara's right wrist and pulled it up for his inspection. Clara swiped her other hand out only to have that caught with his other hand. He turned his attention to the other arm as he turned it around to reveal the claw marks running along them. "It can't be possible," he mumbled, dropping her hands and before she could fight him off Caleb had pulled up her top in order to look at the bite. Within a day the bite alone would be completely healed, leaving only pale scars that would last a lifetime. Yet, bitten strays took a week or more until they were healed enough to Change for the first time. However, the way Clara was healing she would be ready to Change within a matter of hours. "Strays don't heal that quickly," he said pulling her top back down to retain her modesty.

"Like hell they don't, I've watched your kind heal," Clara argued back pulling herself away from him. Her eyes stayed defiantly on his, "The next time you touch me without permission I will rip the offending limb from your body" she growled at him.

Caleb stepped back with his hands palms up to show he meant no harm. Clara stayed growling as she stood up and righted herself. Caleb wondered over the fact that she didn't back down when dealing with him. Most Lycans couldn't even speak back let alone make eye contact with him but Michael, and now Clara, were the exceptions.

"Is she well enough to walk around?" Caleb asked Peter, merely out of politeness even though he knew that she was.

"Perfectly," Peter sighed.

"Good," Caleb looked at Clara, "Time for you to answer some questions"

CHAPTER 3

Clara sat uncomfortably in an armchair facing four male Lycans, one of which was in wolf form. Taking in the fact, that apart from Caleb, it was Michael and Edmund sitting opposite Clara assumed that it was Leonard by Caleb's feet. Unease filled her. Sitting in front of them was like a painful interview that was getting exceedingly worse through its silence. Her mind told her to stay still and act like she was confident and comfortable in this situation, yet another primal part of her was telling her that she was cornered and that it was a choice of running or attacking. Her eyes darted to the closed door. There was no way she could get there and out of the house without one of them grabbing her. Her knee bounced up and down as she thought of running. She was becoming anxious and impatient, which is not a good combination in a trained killer.

They were watching her, assessing her reactions. Clara knew how it went with the board back at The Headquarters; they assessed your body language and worked out visual weaknesses. The difference with Lycans was that they studied everything; changes in scents, body language, and the underlying emotions within a person as well as the weakness that they could see straight away. That's what made them the most difficult to deal with. Even after all her training, Clara now found herself struggling to keep her body under control. She knew how to work around her aggression towards Lycans and make them believe it was lust, but she had no idea how to trick them into believing her anxiety was anything other than anxiety.

"Are you going to ask questions or just stare?" she snapped crossing her arms and legs. Her eyes narrowed on them as she settled on trying to convince them she was angry. It didn't quite work as her right leg kept bouncing up and down nervously.

"I was quite enjoying view," Michael joked. His joke won him a thump on the back from Caleb and a deathly glare from Clara.

"We want to know what happened, just before you were bitten," Caleb stated without looking at her.

"Then ask your questions," Clara stated watching him closely.

"Why were you in Ash Forest?" Caleb asked, mimicking her body language. Crossed arms on him just made him seem more imposing.

"Hunting," she replied not going into details.

"What or who were you hunting?" He pushed.

"Brandon Cox," she replied with a name. The wolf by Caleb raised its head and chuffed. Its tongue flopped to the side of its mouth. He was obviously happy with the news.

"Now that's where we are slightly confused," Michael leaned forwards, his joking smiling turning into a serious straight line. "Cox hadn't harmed anyone, made anyone aware of our existence, and he had never turned anyone. So why were you hunting him?" he asked. Clara's eyes widened. She had never questioned why she gained the targets she had been given, she merely hunted them and killed them.

"I...I never asked. I was merely given his file and told to hunt him" she replied shyly. She looked down into her lap as she thought about it.

She couldn't count how many Lycans she had killed under orders on both hands. The last time she had thought about it, even felt guilty about it, was during her first year in the field. She had only been eighteen and fresh faced after only two years in training. Training had been easy. You focused on dummies or already dead Lycans in a monstrous half-animal forms. In reality Clara had never pictured them looking just like ordinary people. It wasn't until she met Howard and James, who had told her horrifying stories about them, did she even start to think of them as beasts. They became monsters in her mind, and that helped to make them easy to kill.

But now she was one of them and the last man she had killed may not have been guilty of anything, except being a Lycan. Her eyes lifted slightly to look at the men opposite. Apart from Edmund, none of them scared or horrified her. None of them were beasts. They had saved her from death. They had helped her with her only life goal, to survive, unlike Howard who had been the only one to truly know the real her.

"You expect us to believe you never questioned your orders?" roared Edmund. Instinctively Clara's head shot up. Horror filled her eyes. She cowered back into the soft cushioning of the chair. Her arms unfolded and braced the arms of the chair. The child in her readied itself for the hit, the slap that always came when the 'Father' didn't believe her.

"I learnt not to," Clara replied meekly. Her wide eyes watched Edmund carefully. For the first time in a long time, she couldn't control her reactions. He scared her, just as so many foster fathers had.

"Moving on," Caleb interjected putting an arm in front of Edmund. That mere action calmed Clara, although her eyes stayed watched Edmund. "Looking at our information on you, you never failed a mission. What went wrong?" he asked.

"I'm not quite sure," She replied trying to become professional, yet the wariness inside her kept her sounding like a scared young girl rather than a confident woman. "It started off like any hunt. I would lure the stray away from public view or even track them into the woods where they would usually run," she paused and lowered her gaze to her lap once more. Memories of the fight filled her mind. "Someone must have tipped him off," she added, her eyes filling in unwept tears, "Usually it's a clean shot. One to the back of the head, they never even realise. It's a quick death." A sigh past her lips, "But he suddenly disappeared into the branches. I've never seen a Lycan do that, not in my six years in the field…"

"It's unusual," Michael commented, listening to her with intent.

"I couldn't see him, and he jumped down at me. He had shifted completely with claws and fangs out when he attacked. If I hadn't had my gun in my hand there was no way I was getting out of it alive, not against a Lycan in wolf form."

"But you almost didn't get out of it alive." Edmund sneered, "You were shot in the chest"

Clara's eyes narrowed on him. Howard had shot her. He had left her for dead, leaving to her bleed out instead of shooting her again to the head for a finishing blow which would have made sure she was dead. That was the protocol, and the fact he had shot her showed that nothing stood in his way of following the rules. But he had left her to suffer, he had bent the rules. He took some sort of revenge on her and let her bleed out. Her teeth gritted together. Anger filled her. Edmund had reminded her of the one thing she wanted to forget. Who wouldn't want to forget that the one person you thought you could trust shooting you? Her hands balled into fists. "Who shot you?" Edmund asked pushing the subject.

"Who gives a shit," Clara growled back.

"Did you shoot yourself or did someone else?" he pushed again.

"Who cares!" She roared, "I'm alive now. I'm surviving now. So, it doesn't matter who shot me".

Within a blink, Edmund was leaning over her. His eyes stayed on her wide eyes. Clara had sunk further back into the chair, her sharp tongue forgotten. Now she truly was a cornered animal. It was fight or flight.

"You shot yourself, didn't you?" He spat at her. "You didn't ask questions about your targets, probably followed all the rules too"

"Don't make assumptions about…" She replied meekly.

"You did it, didn't you?" He shouted down at her.

"Edmund!" shouted Caleb.

"You hated the thought of being one of us…"

"Get away from me," Clara ordered quietly, her eyes stayed on his.

"To you, we are mere creatures, aren't we? Things you can never regret killing because we are your nightmares. So, you shot yourself, to save yourself the misery of living like one of us".

"Edmund, sit down!" roared Caleb.

"Or did you get a follow hunter to shoot you? You probably didn't have the guts to kill yourself, too cowardly at the core. You probably showed them the bite and prayed for death".

Clara's head tilted. Her eyes burned and her lip twitched. She had only been called a coward only once in her life. One foster mother had called her a coward for not standing up for herself against bullies at school. So, she stopped backing down, even if she wanted to deep down. Clara started fighting back, against bullies, foster parents and anyone that tried to assert control over her.

"Get the fuck away from me" She practically whispered, yet it was as cutting as a knife. A pressure filled the room, her eyes had turned golden.

Slowly Edmund pulled away as she followed his movements. He took a step back as she stood. Her eyes watched him. But Clara was no longer the human hunter. No, she was now thinking and acting like a wolf. She took him in with a curious gaze. The skin around her eyes darkened and morphed in to animalistic golden eyes that absorbed every detail they could see. "If I had shot myself, I wouldn't be standing here" she said ever so calmly, yet her whole body showed her anger. All the pain she had suffered in life shone in those burning bright eyes. Being a hunter had given her meaning but not a true outlet. Now it was biting back. Her horrid memories and the burning fury she had buried deep down were rising with the beast inside.

"Clara, please," Caleb responded holding a protective arm over Edmund, "sit back down".

"I'm done with your questions" she responded.

"No, this is my…"

"I don't care" she responded looking at Caleb.

His eyes morphed to copy her own. This time Clara understood why they kept eye contact. It was all power play. Who would be in charge and who would bow out in defeat. "This is my territory," his calm voice seemed to boom off the walls.

"And you let one of your own threaten me by invading my space," she growled back. Caleb stood, his height should have made her feel a twinge of submission, but instead she stood firm.

"Edmund leave the room," Caleb ordered.

"She is insane," Edmund commented without moving.

"Leave!" Caleb roared. Edmund yelped and scampered from the room. "There your threat is gone. Calm down" he ordered.

Although Clara no longer felt threatened it didn't stop the anger that had boiled over. She couldn't stop it. It blinded her and controlled her. Her hand swiped out catching Caleb off guard. Her still human nails merely grazed the skin it hit. He stayed still and watched her. Her heart pounded in her chest. The bite on her side burnt her side. "Don't tell me what to do!" she roared at him.

"I'm trying to help you" he replied calmly.

"Help me? Help me?" She laughed, "You merely helped yourself. Females are extinct, you only saved me because I'm rare. I'm just the only fucking she-wolf around" her voice started to fade. Her anger slowly diminished. She hadn't been saved by someone who had known her. She hadn't been saved because someone cared. No, she had been saved because she was physically good to keep around. She had survived so long only to be saved for someone else's use.

Tears were falling down her face. Her body shook. She hadn't cried in front of anyone in years, not since she was a child. "Why was it you?" she yelled at him. There was no real anger in her voice. Caleb moved towards her; his arms were out ready to comfort her. "Don't touch me," she cried. He stopped where he was and just watched her. Her fist shot out at his chest, but there was no strength behind it. "Why the fuck was it you?" she wailed as she continued to throwing punches as his chest, "Why wasn't it him? Why did he have to…" her voice became inaudible as she slumped against Caleb.

Caleb stroked her hair and calmly wrapped his arms around her without saying a word. Yet, he looked towards Leo and Michael who had stayed exactly where they were. Michael's eyes were filled with his own memories. Leo, however, lay down watching the scene with distress. Their protective instincts kept them there, wanting to protect the small woman from the horrors that only she knew. Caleb focused his hearing on the rest of the house. Edmund was pacing up and down the hallway while his wife, Mary, was trying to calm him and lecture him at the same time.

"You can't pretend to understand how they think, Eddy" Mary pleaded.

"She's a hunter, a human hunter" he stated back, "They kill us. They are murderers who see us as nothing more than another number to add to their list. They hate us, so of course they would hate to become one of us".

"I want you to calm down and listen, Edmund Kiel" Mary ordered, sounding like an angry mother scolding a young child. "Listen to what is going on in the other room". Edmund's pacing stopped and only Mary's foot tapping could be heard. "Does that sound like someone who hates your kind, our kind?" Mary said making sure to include herself in the Pack even though she was human.

"She could be crying because she was turned," Edmund stated stubborn.

"You stubborn idiot!" Mary shouted at her husband, "I haven't got your increased hearing or keen eye-sight but even I can tell that that woman is not crying because she was turned or hates your kind. She's a trained hunter, do you not think that her 'Plan B' would have been to attack all of you?" Silence filled the house except for Clara's sobs. "You know I'm right," Mary added.

Clara pulled away from Caleb and without lifting her head, she headed out of the room. Her eyes landed on the now quiet couple standing just outside the door. Edmund no longer stood at his full height, instead his shoulders hung forwards and any anger that was once in his person was gone. Mary, however, put on a smile and stepped towards Clara. "You must be exhausted from dealing with them, I know I always am. How about I show you to the spare room?" Mary inquired without sparing Caleb or Michael a glance to make sure that was okay.

"That...Is that..." Clara stuttered trying to form the sentence.

"We can't expect you stay sleeping in the medical room, the whole time you are here," Mary giggled trying to make Clara feel more comfortable. "I already sorted out sheets, towels and anything else you would need for one night," Mary paused, "and tomorrow we can go shopping to find you some other clothes to wear. I'm sure you must be tired of wearing those ripped up old things".

Looking down at herself, Clara suddenly felt subconscious. "That would be nice, I guess," She answered with a timid smile. Mary wrapped an arm around Clara's waist and ushered her up the stairs.

"You'll like it here," Mary said softly as they disappeared from the men's views, "They are hard to deal with sometimes, and you must understand why they want to know about why you were shot and even living for that matter".

"I understand," Clara replied as they walked into a small cosy bedroom. Mary settled her on her bed carefully and stepped back smiling.

"You know, I always wanted another woman around here who actually liked being around the boys," Mary whispered softly, "There's a few more of them, a couple of them are even married with children. But their wives don't like visiting that often, they like to pretend their husbands aren't different."

"But they know?" Clara questioned her. She had never come across Lycans having families. She had known some were born, so they had to have families at some point. But she just figured the women never truly knew, or at least that was what Howard had guessed.

"Of course, they know," Mary was shocked by the question, "Why wouldn't they know?" Clara stayed quiet. "Anyway, I hope you like it here because I could use another pair of hands to help me to deal with the men on an everyday basis. They're not bad, they just tend to be a bit obtuse towards the female nature, if you get my meaning". Clara just nodded even though she had no idea about 'The female nature', and if it had anything to do with how women operate, she was pretty sure that she couldn't really speak on that matter.

Mary took the nod as the end of the conversation and smiled her goodbyes. Slowly and without turning around she walked out of the room and closed the door. Clara listened as Mary's footsteps disappeared down the stairs.

Suddenly she was torn between investigating the room she had been given and going to sleep. Her body longed for rest whilst her mind wanted to roam. So, she settled for lying down on the bed and just looking around her which seemed to be a good compromise as her body was already aching. She noted that the light from the window shone onto the right side of the double bed she had been given and a decent sized wooden wardrobe stood the wall opposite the end of her bed. The room itself was barely furnished. It had a bed, a wardrobe, a desk with a chair, and a couple of bedside tables. There was no clutter or any sign of the room belonging to anyone before her.

Satisfied that the room was adequate and that she was at least safe for the night, she tugged her jeans off and shrugged off her top. Gently she pulled the covers up and slid underneath them. Warmth enveloped her and settled a deeper wilder part of her. Her eyes drifted shut with the thought that she would live another day.

CHAPTER 4

The night's sleep hadn't been an easy one. Her eyes kept flickering open as her mind reminded her was what happened. Sometimes the dreams would be warm and loving but soon enough a nightmare involving Howard would creep in. He would be standing there with the barrel of the gun aimed at her. Each time his face held a different expression, but it didn't change the fact that every time her mind flung the nightmare at her it scared her so much that she woke up. A scream never escaped her, but there was a strange and almost suffocating scent in the room that her mind registered as fear. However, as soon as sunlight hit the window her mind settled enough to allow her to sleep soundlessly.

At ten in the morning after just five hours of decent sleep, Clara finally woke up. Her body still ached but it no longer bothered her. Slowly she turned to her left and stared at the bedroom door. She was surprised to find that she wasn't scared or frightened by the fact she was in a new unknown place, instead she was content by the fact she was surrounded by others which was something she had never felt before. Still, she told herself to stay weary and to keep an eye on everyone here.

Slowly she raised herself from her bed, her body argued with every movement she made. As she stood, she became painfully aware of the fact that she could sense everyone downstairs. In her own chest she could feel the steady and calm rhythms of their hearts, as well as feel their breathing patterns. As they walked around or sat down, she felt their movements in her own muscles. Shaking her head Clara tried to ignore the attachment her body seemed to have formed to the people around. Instead of focusing on the sensations in her body she quickly put her torn clothing back on and headed out of the bedroom.

Once she was in the hallway, she walked straight to the bathroom. She had no idea how she knew which door was which as they were all shut, but it was something strange that she chose to ignore. Clara quickly undressed after she locked the door and climb in under the hot spray of the shower. The hot clean water seemed to wash everything away, from the dirt that still covered her body to the worries that lay deep within her mind. Rolling her shoulders Clara turned and stared at the tile wall as water cascaded down her back. In the bright light she could see only an essence of her reflection in the tile, yet something felt like everything fitted perfectly now. The hazy woman that stared back at her felt whole.

Turning off the shower, Clara stepped out and grabbed the nearest towel. She wrapped it around her and then wiped the mirror free of any fog. As the mist was wiped away a small gasp fell from her lips. She looked different just as much as she felt different. The face staring back of her was the same, but there was now something deeper within her own eyes. A golden circle lined her pupil, whilst her skin seemed less worn. Her hand stayed gently resting against the mirror as she focused on her eyes. The skin around them had darkened slightly making it seem like she had just put on eyeliner, yet she knew for certain that she hadn't. Leaning forwards her gaze turned to the hand on the mirror. Her nails were longer and much more pointed, like blunted claws.

Quickly she pulled herself away and hurriedly got dried off then dressed once again. Stilling for a moment, she eyed the door. Her pulse should have risen with shock or distress and yet she found herself calming to the same rate as everyone in the house. Breathing in, she stepped out of the bathroom and into the hallway. Without hesitation she walked downstairs, yet her blue eyes watched every exit possible as she walked down. Clara stilled as she reached the bottom step and eyed the open door to the kitchen. There were no sounds coming from any of the rooms that hinted that anyone was around, and yet in her own muscles and mind she knew that everyone was seated in the study which she had been questioned in the day before. Swallowing hard, she made her way to the door that lay between her and everyone else. A part of her wanted to rush in and enjoy the company which they had to offer yet another side, a stronger side, told to wait and listen.

So, she did, Clara stood by the door listening to the almost silent sounds of their breathing.

Her right hand hovered of the door handle. She knew in her body that they were calm and were waiting for her, yet her mind told her to be ready for an attack. She clicked her neck and rolled her shoulders. Pulling sharply down on the handle Clara opened the door and stared at the people who waited for her.

She looked at every one of them individually, her eyes took note of their body language, their scents and even where they sat. Michael was the only one who stood in the room. Clara knew instantly that he was the Enforcer of the Pack's rulings, whilst Caleb sat on the furthest side of the group from her. Something in her mind told her that he was in the position of power. The path to him wasn't blocked by anyone but lined by the others. Leonard and Edmund sat on either of Caleb, whilst Mary was seated next to Edmund and was almost within reach. Clara turned her gaze to the closed curtains. The light that shone through the gap shimmered off various sources, instantly she knew that there was more to the Pack than those she had met the day before.

A figure moved from the shadows in the room to stand alongside Michael, proving their equal standing. Compared to Michael's gentle giant appearance, the man who now stood next to him was the personification of wrath. His eyes didn't match in colour, one was gold whilst the other had a human green. His body was bulkier making him looked stronger than anyone else who she could see in the room. Scars marked his face, whilst dark hair fell to around his shoulders. Clara only hoped his temperament differed from his appearance.

"Did I interrupt something?" Clara asked as she leaned against the wall opposite them all, knowing full well that the group had been silent all morning.

"Take a seat," ordered Leonard as he gestured to the empty space next to him. Clara just shrugged and flipped an extra light switch that highlighted the rest of the room. Looking around from where she stood, she eyed the other three men that had been standing in the shadows of the room. They were nothing special.

To her they looked like the generic recruits The Order would hire to do their dirty work. All of them were fit and healthy, with height that would rival some of the men she had met in her lifetime, and seemingly matching shades of brown hair. Only their scents differed. Clara eyes widened slightly as her mind told her of that difference.

"Please take a seat," Leonard pushed again, the urgency in his eyes pulled at her sympathy but it did little else.

"I'm happy to stand," Clara replied turning her gaze to the two Enforcers that stood by Caleb. Michael was smiling to himself whilst the other was brooding over something. "Are you going to tell me why you've been in here all morning?" she pushed feeling slightly unsettled by the fact everyone's eyes were on her.

"We wanted to meet the only female to exist in the past fifty years," stated one of the three unknown men, "especially as she was once a killer of our kind". Clara turned on him. Her eyes took his appearance in a much greater detail. The man looked a little older than herself, yet something told her that he had lived for many more years than he appeared to be. His hair was dirt brown with a small patch of grey by his left ear. A small number of whiskers along his jaw hinted that he hadn't shaved for at least twelve hours. Her mind started to list things about him she couldn't possibly know from just a close inspection. Like the fact he favoured his left leg hinted at a recent injury to his right leg, and that his hands kept flexing which showed he had held back some anger when speaking to her, or the fact that something in his scent told her that he was confused and all of his emotions were on a high making him the most volatile in the room.

Being the woman she was, Clara just smiled at him. Something in her brain told her that she was baring her teeth, but she didn't care. "How's the leg?" she asked sweetly gaining a growl of displeasure in return.

"I'm sure you would know about that, wouldn't you?" he growled in returned. Clara instantly knew he had had a run in with a hunter a short while ago. Her head tilted looking directly at his leg. The most basic attack a hunter would pull is to trap a Lycan in wolf form with a silver laced trap.

"Was it basic silver twine or a snapper?" she asked intrigued by the fact he had escaped the trap mostly in one piece. Most Lycans were trapped in them for hours, or if they were stupid enough only for a few minutes because they thought to sneak up on the hunter. "Or maybe you were lucky enough to only get a shot to the leg instead of getting caught in a trap?" She added keeping her voice sweet and innocent sounding.

He growled back in returned but stayed where he was. Something inside her reprimanded her for her words and told her she was meant to stay pleasant towards this people, but something new felt victorious for finding a true and useable weakness.

"Enough," ordered Caleb, causing everyone to turn their gaze to him. Clara was the last one turn to him and the only one to meet his dark eyes with her own. "I called you all here to meet Clara and to discuss bringing her into the Pack, permanently" his voice carried throughout the room. A growl past Clara's lips, as something inside her told her she had a rightful place in the Pack without their consent. "Something wrong?" Caleb questioned narrowing his gaze.

"Nothing," Clara said, although the bitter taste of a lie sank into her mouth causing her to practically chock on it. A side of her was lying, that side of her hated the fact they didn't instantly welcome her into their fold. That side of her believe she was above all of them, except the man who sat on the furthest side of the room.

"Are you sure something isn't wrong?" Michael pushed, causing her to look towards him. His eyes were full of sympathy as if he knew the anguish going on in her mind.

"No, I'm fine," she growled out, once again she started to choke from the bitter taste of a lie. Suddenly she was aware of everyone staring at her. She felt like she was under attack, they were looking for weakness, for anything that they could use against her. Her skin itched and a rumble echoed from her chest. "Stop staring at me!" she bellowed through her growl.

Caleb watched as Clara struggled to hide the changes happening to her. She choked on every lie that left her mouth, because she hadn't worked out which side of herself to listen to. Her body gradually bent over as she struggled to lie. Her mind and body were struggling with the other side of the Bite. Usually the toxins took longer to take full effect. It would start with heightened hearing, then over a matter of days the person's sight and smell with gradually increase. It was all barely noticeable. Then over the space of a week they would experience a problem with lying, hiding their emotions, and start to notice the unnoticeable in people around them. Yet Clara was showing all of those symptoms now, only after two days of being bitten. Her body was accepting the poison too quickly.

Suddenly her head lifted. Her once sky-blue eyes were now pure gold. Her lips were pulled back to reveal that her canines had lengthened and seemed sharper. The tips of her fingers were clawed. "Stop staring at me!" she growled. Power filled the room. Everyone looked anywhere but her except Michael, Caleb and the broody Joseph. Alarm bells rang in Caleb's mind. She shouldn't have even been close to shifting for another week at the least. No human changed this quickly. No woman ever survived the bite, the poison killed them instantly, and yet the one in front of him had survived the initial contact with the poison and was now going through an accelerated Change, which even born wolf didn't go through the first time.

Her eyes closed and a groan escaped her. Caleb stood up and slowly made his way towards her. "Get away from me!" she roared stopping him in his tracks. The one that spoke now wasn't the human woman, but the creature born from her spirit. Her golden eyes opened and glared at him. There was no malice or anger he thought that he would see in them. Instead it was fear that shone out. The wolf was acting as it was outnumbered and being attack from all sides.

Instantly Caleb held his arms out with his palms facing her as he lowered himself so that he knelt before her. The others in the room lowered themselves as not to hold their heads higher than his. "We're not going to hurt you," he said softly to her, trying to reassure the beast within.

"Get away from me!" Clara roared again before a deafening scream of pain escaped her. Her knees met the ground and her head fell forwards. Her clawed hands scratched at the hard wood floor. Caleb could do nothing to help and found himself struggling to watch the woman go through something that came naturally to every man in the room.

Michael rushed forwards, ignoring the growls that escaped Caleb. He quickly ripped the t-shirt from Clara's body then created a tear at the clasp of her bra and the waistline of her jeans. "What do you think you are doing?" yelled Mary, shocked at the fact Michael had practically undressed a woman in a room full of men.

"If she Changes in her clothes, she will strangle herself to death" Michael pushed causing Mary to gasp and lean into Edmund. Michael moved behind Caleb and stayed standing. If Clara's animal side attacked blindly as soon as she shifted, he would have to put her down.

The sounds of bones cracking filled the room. Clara's fingers cracked as the bones moved in to new positions. The flesh fattened and started to take shape. Her body moved quickly as fur radiated from the base of her neck downwards. Instantly her head shot up. The nose and jaw were lengthening. A whine escaped her as more bones cracked into their new places. Whatever clothing had been left on her body tore off her transforming body. Fur now covered her fully. Finally, a tail grew, and her golden eyes opened.

A honey-coloured she-wolf stood before them with no sign of human rationality in her almost camouflaged eyes. It snapped its jaws together bearing its deadly fangs in warning. All of them watched as the she-wolf tried to push herself further and further into the wall. Her whole body was shaking. The blinding scent of fear and anger bellowed to life in the room. No one moved. No one spoke. All of them watched the she-wolf.

Michael instantly stepped closer. He knew every sign she was giving off extremely well. His own half-brother had shown the same symptoms. His brother had lived his life with an abusive step-father and mother before Michael's father had found him. The spirit inside him had been beaten, broken and abused beyond belief. Clara was snapping and growling as she tried to back away. Her body shook with fear. Her eyes watched everyone; the wolf knew it was outnumbered even if it somehow knew no one was going to attack her.

"Everyone leave the room," Michael ordered without looking at the crowd of spectators. No one answered back as they slowly and silently left the room. The she-wolf watched them closely. Michael looked towards Caleb, "You have to shift," he stated as he tried to hold back the memories of his own brother. "You have to shift and convince the wolf it doesn't need to protect its human side".

"She just shifted; it'll take a little while to…" Caleb tried to argue back.

"Just change!" Michael ordered. His eyes glowed in his anger and frustration. Caleb took note of the fact that his subordinate wolf had just given him an order, which had never happened before, he nodded and braced himself to shift.

Caleb pulled his shirt up over his head and quickly stripped off his jeans before letting his wolf take over. In a blink of an eye his wolf stood facing the growling she-wolf. He was at least a head taller than her with black and brown mottled fur. The she-wolf snapped her jaws and growled at him as he stood mere inches away from her. He slowly lowered his head slightly, so he didn't tower over her. The she-wolf flicked her tongue nervously eyeing the rest surrounding her. Caleb stepped closely nudging her with his nose in a friendly greeting. She grumbled but allowed it. He pushed further forwards brushing his muzzle against hers before placing his head on top of her. A grumble left her, but it stilled.

Shortly she rubbed her muzzle against his before stepping closer. The wolf eyed the others, but her growling had ceased until her eyes landed on Edmund. Michael moved to stand in her way of sight, but the wolf shot past him towards Edmund. She launched herself at him until she stood over him as his chair toppled back onto the floor. She growled and bared her teeth at him. Her tongue peeked out as if tasting the air around him. Caleb hurried over to her and shoved his head under hers to shove her back. She snapped and wriggled against his hold. He gave up and stood up over her. He bit down on the back of her neck causing her to yelp and struggle to get away. As he released her, the she-wolf back away and rolled over on the floor trying to appease him. Caleb licked her muzzle and walked away back to his clothes.

The she-wolf sat up and watched him shift back but made no movement to follow suit.

CHAPTER 5

It took twelve hours for the wolf to show any sign of human consciousness and another two days until Clara finally shifted back. This gave Mary the perfect amount of time to go clothes shopping for Clara without any arguments over what she picked out. The closest she got to an argument was Clara grumbling as Mary showed her each garment. The other upside is that Clara could watch everyone without them knowing what she was thinking. She watched and listened to every conversation amongst the pack members. Some whispered about why Caleb was being blinded about her crimes against their kind, whilst the majority couldn't believe how she stood up against Caleb or how she had shifted so fast after being bitten. But no one threatened her existence or seemed wary of her presence.

Finally feeling safe around most of the people in the house, Clara went up to her room and pushed herself to shift back. She stayed on the floor with eyes closed trying to work out how for a couple of hours. The wolf within seemed to take pity on her and eased back. When she shifted back Clara changed into loose summer dress which Mary had deemed too cute to turn down. Clara looked at herself in the mirror. The last time she had worn a dress had been when she was fifteen and way before she joined The Order. She smoothed out invisible creases and brushed out her hair. She felt like a different person although she wasn't sure whether dresses suited her.

Barefooted she walked downstairs and walked straight into the kitchen where Mary was preparing lunch for everyone. "What are you making?" Clara asked catching Mary off guard. Wide-eyed Mary turned seeing Clara in human form and grinned.

"Oh, I'm so happy you changed back. I was starting to think you were going to stay like that," Mary gushed before pulling Clara into a strong embrace. Clara stood stock still as the small woman hugged her, it was something she wasn't used to. All her life she had to earn affection and praise; she wasn't quite sure how she had earned Mary's affection.

"Well, don't you look good when you're not growling and covered in blood," said a deep voice from the doorway. Clara turned to see Michael leaning against the door frame. Mary released Clara and waved her finger at Michael, "Where were you when I needed help in the garden earlier?" she lectured him.

"Caleb asked me…"

"You listen to me young man. Caleb may be your alpha, but I keep this house running, if I ask you to do chores you come running" Mary said sternly. Clara stifled a giggle and perched herself up at the countertop. For the past day she had watched Mary fling wooden spoons at Michael when he hadn't listened to her and even drag Leonard away by the ear when he tried to chat up the pizza delivery girl. It was refreshing to see after Clara had spent years picturing shifters as monsters since she started her training, and here they were being lectured by a five-foot-nothing woman as if they were no more than unruly children.

Mary turned back to her food preparation as Michael cosied up to Clara, "She's nice now but wait until you spill wine on her favourite table cloth" he joked.

"I only yelled at you because you did it on purpose," Mary argued back without turning around.

"and tried to blame it on me, if I remember correctly" Caleb said as he walked in from the garden.

Clara watched him closely as he walked in with low rise jeans on and his T-shirt flung over his shoulder. "The building work you wanted done is almost finished" Caleb said with a smile before kissing Mary on the cheek. He turned to Clara and Michael, "Good to see that you shifted back," he grinned before glaring at Michael, "Did you do the research I asked for?"

"Just finished," Michael grinned.

"What research?" Clara asked her eyes flicking between the two.

"To see if you truly are the only she-wolf around," Michael answered.

"And?"

"It seems you're the first in the last fifty years, so the only thing left to do is to work out why," Michael shrugged.

"And how," Clara added solemnly.

"You listen here," Mary shoved Caleb out of the way, "You can stay here as long as you want, even if we find out how you become a Lycan, it doesn't mean we'll no longer want you around. Do you understand?" Mary eyed her closely as Clara just stared at her. The women didn't need a super sniffer or added instincts because she could hint a nail on the head without fully paying attention. How she knew Clara had felt a small distress at the thought of them no longer wanting her around was beyond her.

"Anyway, the fact that you're the only female wolf here, makes you an alpha" Michael grinned over at Caleb, who glared back.

"Alpha?"

"Apart from little old me no one has been able to look Caleb in the eye for longer than a few seconds let alone argue back," he nudged her, "that makes you alpha material".

Clara just stared at them all. She had gone from being just a tool to being almost at the top of a wolf pack in a matter of days. In other words, she mattered. Her fist tightened as she looked down at her lap. Suddenly she felt too awkward and envious. The dress had to go, she had to find something she was used to. Something that made her feel like she used to, confident, in control, and a soldier. She jumped down from her perch and without a word to the others she raced off her to room to search through her clothes.

She threw clothes around the room trying to find anything that resembled what she usually wore. A pair of jeans, a plain t-shirt or something leather but everything had something feminine to do with them. Her breathing became ragged as she struggled to get over everything. She had gone from being just a grunt and someone's on-and-off relationship to being someone that could matter to people. She couldn't understand how. She had never truly mattered to anyone since her parents died. The foster home had given up on her after the tenth lot of foster parents handed her back. School hadn't cared if she failed or passed, she just slipped through their system. Then The Order found her, and they wanted her as a weapon. Howard had loved her in his own way but never more than his ingrained rules. That was the reason they broke up so many times. But their jobs kept them too close to get over each other. Now she was in a house where there was at least one person, Mary, who wanted to keep her around for good after just a few days of knowing her. "Give it a week," a memorised voice trickled in her head from a conversation she had overheard at the foster home when she was given to her last foster family, "they'll have enough of her by then".

"Redecorating already?" said a voice from the doorway. Clara looked up to see Caleb walking in looking at the clothes she had thrown across the room.

"I couldn't find something to wear," she answered moving to pick some of the mess up.

"I think you look good in what you've already got on," confusion written on his face.

"It's just not what I'm used to," she whispered shoving thing back in draws.

"What's wrong? You were fine a minute ago," he stated sitting down on her bed. Clara finally looked straight at him. He was still topless as he held his t-shirt in his hands. The beast in her mind told her to go over to him and to rub herself against him. Her eyes widened that the thought and shoved the beast back.

"It just got too much," she answered grabbing some more of her clothes.

Silently he moved behind her catching her off guard when she turned around. Clara was torn between shoving him away and yelling at him or pulling him down so she could kiss him. The beast inside favoured the latter. "You can stay here for as long as you like, we're not going to push you" he repeated what Mary said.

"You don't know me," she answered back, "You'll get sick of me and want to chase me off".

"We'd never do that,"

"You don't know me," she repeated, "And you will".

Caleb's hand shot out grabbing her arm and pulling her to look directly at him, "Did someone do that to you? Chase you off? Who hurt you?" he asked her, watching her eyes closely.

"Let go," she said tugging herself free.

"Will you at least tell me who shot you?" He pleaded.

"My boyfriend," she replied softly before slumping down on her bed putting distance between them.

Caleb couldn't believe his ears. Her boyfriend, someone he guessed she had loved, had shot her when she had been bitten. It was no wonder she thought they would want to get rid of her. "Was he part of The Order?" he queried.

"He was the best hunter, a stickler for the rules," she practically spat, "I was surprised he was even interested in a deviant recruit like me".

"So, you've never been one to follow an authority figure?"

"They never gave me a reason to follow," she replied leaned back on her bed.

"You don't like going into detail, do you?" Caleb smiled as he sat down next to her.

"A skill I picked up at my foster homes, no one can blame things on you if you can rewrite the truth" she grinned at him.

"A survivor at heart,"

"Always had to be," she said grimly before sitting up. Her hands gripped his forearm as she turned to him, "I want to get one thing out in the open. I never joined The Order because I hated Shifters, I never even knew they existed. I was a nobody when they found me, just a lost child. They noticed me and saw their chance at having a recruit with no attachments. I didn't even hate shifters when I first started hunting. I just distanced my emotions from the process and learnt that it was a necessary evil. They helped me learn skills that have helped me survive. In this whole world I am on my own, and the only thing I knew I could do well was survive."

"Now you have us," he replied, "Even if you leave, you are in this Pack which means you have a family".

Clara blinked at him. He smiled softly at her. Her heart raced as the beast inside was raging to get out. The human side was too stunned at what he said to stop the she-wolf. Clara's hand shot out grabbing Caleb and pulled him towards her. Their lips met but the she-wolf wanted more. One of Caleb's hands rested against her neck urging her to tilt her head up whilst his other arm anchored her against him. Her mouth opened with a moan and his tongue dove in. Their tongues dance as they clung to each other. Caleb quickly realised what had happened and slowly pulled away from her. Clara sat just starting at him with golden eyes. "I…I'm sorry" she muttered leaning away from him. Caleb noted how she shook her head trying to dislodge something. He breathed in catching scent of the she-wolf just below her skin, and something his wolf wanted claim as his. And he wasn't someone not to listen to his wolf.

Caleb pulled her back to him, "Don't be," he whispered before kissing her again. He felt her soften against him as she wrapped her arms around his neck. Her clawed nails gripped his shoulder pulling him with her as she leaned back. Her teeth nipped his bottom lip and her eyes flickered open as he pulled back slightly. Her eyes glowed gold as her wolf sat calmly behind them. Clara lightly ran her claws down his torso admiring the muscles that tensed beneath her touch. The wolf blocked every thought that rested in her mind, everything that didn't revolve around the man before her. Something about him made the she-wolf want to rub herself all over him. He leaned back down kissing her lightly on the cheek before moving further down her neck. Her hands moved to his neck and she closed her eyes. She could feel his heart beat, could sense his attraction and lust, and she couldn't feel and scent anything but him. His fingers danced along her sides gripping the thin fabric of her dress. Possessively her wolf took over. She pulled him back up and claimed his lips in a deep passion-filled kiss. She wrapped her legs around his hips before turning them over until she was on top.

Once perched on top she sat back and just looked down at him. Caleb was handsome with golden eyes that watched her closely and a smile that urged her to take things further. "Mine" growled a voice in her head causing Clara to jump back away from Caleb. What had she been doing? He wasn't hers; she had barely known him for a week. This wolf thing was sending her hormones crazy. She shouldn't be looking at other men, she had to be reeling from Howard's betrayal. That must be what caused her to seek comfort. That's all it was, just her seeking comfort from the first kind man who got close enough.

Caleb sat up and watched as she paced around the room trying to work something out. He stayed quiet, unsure as to what had just happened. He had listened to his wolf and he knew that this female in front of him was what his wolf wanted. Clara turned looked at him, her eyes turning from back and forth between blue and gold as she battled between the two parts of her soul now. He shuffled himself forwards, so he was just perched on the edge of the bed. She stepped closer and her eyes turned gold again. She stepped forwards until she stood between his legs. Her eyes watched his. "Why does this feel right?" she asked softly watching her fingers draw invisible patterns on his chest. "The beast keeps pushing me closer to you and it feels right but it shouldn't, should it?" she queried looking up at him.

Caleb's hands moved to hold her against him, and he looked up at her. "This happens sometimes," he said, "It used to happen all the time when she-wolves were common."

"There used to be more?" she said leaning back to look at down at him properly.

"About a hundred years ago there were just as many females as there were males," he smiled before returning to her original question, "The wolf side is usually dormant and helps us along with everyday things by giving us extra abilities, and it only fights for control when the individual has become too uncontrollably anger or when the wolf wants someone. The latter only happens once in a lifetime".

Clara quietened and stepped back from him. "Did it work?" she asked without looking at him.

"Most of the time," he said turning to her.

Slowly she eased out of his embrace and moved to tidy her room again. It wasn't right to feel instantly attached to someone after one kiss. She had barely settled into being a Lycan. Maybe this was something like Stockholm syndrome. That she only felt attached to him because he had saved her, looked after her and was kind to her. "Don't over think it," she heard him say softly as he watched her. She swallowed hard; the she-wolf wanted to be next to him.

"This is so fast, why is everything happening so fast?" she stated dropping what she was moving. Her eyes turned to him. "I shifted within a day, I only just shifted back after adjusting to my wolf form and then this" she waved her hand between the two of them, "My wolf won't shut up and it's happening so fast. She there, in my mind, as if she has always been there. I can feel her but it's no different to before, her voice is just louder." Clara put her head in her hands, "I don't understand this."

"What do you mean it's no different to before?" Caleb asked trying to pull her back to him, even if he was only able to touch her hand. He needed to feel her skin as if to reassure himself she was still there.

"I've always been able to hear people nearby, sense their presence and have even had keen eyesight, it's just enhanced a little now. I've always been more animalistic and instinctive compared to others, that's why I never stayed with families too long. The wolf just…well, she… it feels like she isn't new, just louder as if I've never listened to her before". Clara stared up at Caleb.

"We'll work this out, okay?" Caleb said grabbing her hand.

Clara pulled her hand out of his hold. "I just need space. This is too fast, too confusing" she pleaded him gazing up at his dark brown eyes. How she wanted to push the rational side of her brain away and just give in to the animal within that tried to stretch beneath her skin.

"Okay," Caleb said bowing his head, "When you need us, you know where to find us".

Clara watched him leave her in her room. Loneliness filled her almost pushing her to go after him, to say hell with it all but she couldn't. She barely knew him. Sure, she had watched him these past few days as she wandered around in her new wolf skin, but she didn't know him. He was so similar to Howard in the way he could command a room just by entering, but unlike Howard he was warm, friendly and playful without her having to tease it out of him. Clara sat down on her bed with her head in her hands. She was lost and had no idea how she was going to survive.

CHAPTER 6

The Order

Howard Jones stood before the Council who had been in a gathering for over a week now. No one had known that he had had a relationship with Clara, all they knew is that his occasional work partner had been killed during a mission. The Order wasn't sentimental over these things. As he stayed quiet watching the Council members talk amongst themselves, he tried to block out the shock he had seen in Clara's face when he shot her. He didn't know whether his shot had killed her or left her suffering for hours, that fact haunted him. He would have put her out of her misery if Natalie hadn't started having a panic attack.

"Agent Jones," called a voice bringing Howard out of his memories.

"Yes, Sir" Howard answered stepping out of the line.

"You may have heard that there have been some disturbing rumours going around lately," stated one of the Council members, Stiles.

"I haven't heard any, sir. I have been busy cleaning up the mess left on my ex-partners mission" Howard answered clenching his fists at his sides.

"And there I thought all Agents kept their ears open to rumours," mumbled another council member, General McKenzie who was Natalie's Grandfather.

"We have heard rumours of a female shifter living a few miles from Ash Forest, in a place called Hartwick." stated Stiles, ignoring McKenzie.

"There are no female shifters anymore, sir," Howard replied.

"That's why we need you, Agent," Councilman Higham said, "You are to travel to the local pack, the

Daevers' Pack, and ask them questions. If anyone knows of a female shifter it would be the local pack. You are not to attack or kill whilst on their land. The Order's rules must be held in high regard. We cannot afford a war".

"Yes, Sir" Howard stand straighter.

"You are also to take Agent McKenzie with you. It is time she saw the other side of our operations" stated McKenzie.

"We expect you to move out in the next few days," Stile said, "That will be all, Agent Jones.

"Sir" Howard said before marching out.

The doors shut behind him. Air rushed out of his lungs as he realised, he was going to be returning to the area he had left Clara for dead. Straightening his back, he walked towards training room where he knew he would find Natalie.

***

Clara stayed still by the window in her room as a large black SUV pulled up in the drive. Fear gripped her stomach. She watched as the doors opened. A black-haired woman stepped out. Clara caught a glimpse of her face and noted that it was Natalie, the one that had pushed Howard to check Clara's wounds. A growl rumbled in her chest, but it halted at the sight of the second person.

"I told you she would bring The Order here!" yelled a voice downstairs. Edmund was in his usual paranoid rage. Clara no longer cared for his rants; it was just him airing out his fears. It helped him cope, helped him rationalise situations. It didn't mean her inner child no longer feared his behaviour, instead she was getting used to it a little with each day she was here.

"Will you be quiet, Edmund!" yelled Mary in return. There was shuffling downstairs, but Clara no longer cared as she watched the Agents walk towards the door. The man moved with strength and control. Howard always had an air about him that drew everyone's gaze.

The doorbell rang. "I'm not answering that," Edmund spat, Clara could hear him storm into another room. Clara moved slowly out into the landing to hear things better. The front door opened, "Hello?" Mary greeted them.

"Is this the Daever residence?" asked Natalie in her sickly-sweet voice. Clara almost gagged at the sound.

"Who's asking?" Mary replied with a bitterness that made Clara proud.

"We are from The Order," Howard spoke up, causing goose bumps to rise along Clara's arms. "And we've heard of some disturbances in this area, so we have come to check in with your alpha".

"Well, won't you come in," Mary said. Clara heard her moving out of the way and the agents stepping in. "The Alpha is just through those doors," Mary stated pointing them towards the living room opposite the stairs. As they moved towards the room, Clara stalked down the stairs watching the guests closely.

Caleb looked up catching a glimpse of Clara watching from a hidden perch on the stairs. He halted Joseph from closing the living room doors. "Won't you sit," Caleb stated to the Agents before glancing back at Clara. Quickly he moved his focus to the agents in the room. The woman was young with dark skin and black coal eyes that gazed around the room taking in all the men in the room. There was no slight interest in the woman's eyes like most women instead there was pure hate. Her anger oozed from her being as her hand moved to rest on the gun at her hip. The man, however, glared at Caleb knowing he was the most powerful man in the room. On another day, Caleb would have accepted the challenge in the man's eyes. The man opposite was tall, blonde and obviously spent a lot of his time working if that bland expression was anything to go by. Caleb felt the urge to scare him, to send him running for the hills. Instead Caleb relaxed in his chair letting his easy-going mask fall in place. "How can I help you?" he said crossing his arms.

"We have been sent to investigate sightings of a female shifter around here" Howard stated.

"Female shifter?" questioned Edmund, "There hasn't been one for almost fifty years, and women aren't born unless there are both female and males around".

"We all know the mythology," Natalie stated stressing her boredom with the discussion, "Have you heard anything from other shifters?"

"Nothing," Caleb answered trying not to gaze over in Clara's direction.

"Then you won't mind if we look around your place?" Howard asked.

"Actually I do mind, many of my wolf don't favour your kind. I hope you understand that my refusal more to do your safety rather than my privacy," Caleb answered glaring at the man. Clara moved further down the stairs. Caleb caught her movements; he didn't understand why she was moving closer to the room.

Clara came to stand just next to the door to the living room. Her heart pounded. She knew that she should hide upstairs, allow Howard and Natalie stay ignorant of her existence. But she knew The Order would only send more. She would be locked inside the house for the rest of her life. The Order never gave up. So, she would have to face her nightmares right now. Howard would recognise her and realise he hadn't killed her, and Natalie would finally find out how a feral wolf really kills its prey. Anger boiled up within her as she made the small step into the room. Caleb's eyes flashed to her. Clara could see every emotion there. Fear, anger, confusion and something else that she didn't want to work out. "You were looking for me?" Clara said turning her eyes on Howard and Natalie. They turned and their eyes widened.

"Clara…" Howard said softly.

"Surprised?" Clara said feeling the wolf inside getting ready to pounce.

"I…You're dead"

"You know that I've never been able to stay down,"

"You're meant to be dead!" shouted Natalie raising her gun and readied it to shoot.

"You shoot and it's the last thing you do McKenzie!" growled Clara.

"I think you have overstayed your welcome," Michael said moving to stand in front of Clara.

Howard and Natalie were pushed out of the house by the enforcers, but it didn't stop Natalie turning around with venom in her eyes and voice, "The Order will be here soon. You better be willing to give up your freedom for that she-bitch!"

The door shut and Clara was pushed down into the sofa. "What the hell were you thinking?!" Caleb yelled down at her. His body grew as the beast within him wrestled to gain control, to teach the she-wolf who was in charge.

"They killed me!" Clara yelled back.

"They didn't have to know you were still alive!"

"They should suffer with the knowledge that they failed!" Clara said pushing herself up until she was standing toe to toe with Caleb. "It's better that they know now rather than later!"

"You just wanted a fight!"

"So what? Don't I deserve one? Don't I deserve revenge for what they did?!" her voice ricocheted off the walls

"So, they shot you and left you for dead?" Caleb said, "What would have happened if they hadn't done that? You sure as hell wouldn't have gotten out of The Order or have met us?!"

"Oh, so I'm meant to be grateful to them?!" Clara growled shoving at his shoulders, "Because without them I wouldn't have gotten here?"

"That's not what I meant"

"Sure, it isn't. They left me for dead! They only person I'm grateful to is you. Not them! Never...."

Clara was so caught up in yelling at him that she became utterly shocked when Caleb's mouth lowered on hers. His arms wrapped around her pulling her against him. Clara's hands sat flat against his chest whilst his hands moved to grip the back of her head. His fingers brushed through her hair as his tongue dominated her mouth.

The wolf inside pushed against Clara's skin until she sat just beneath her eyes. Her force caused Clara to wrap her arms around Caleb's neck to deepen their kiss. Her now clawed nails gripped the back of his shoulders. A growl rumbled through Caleb's body as he lifted her up until Clara's leg wrapped around his waist. His lips moved from her mouth to run down her neck. A moan escaped Clara as something hard appeared at her back. The lips and tongue running down her neck and across her collar bone kept her was trying to work out where she was.

A hand moved from holding her up to move between them, a feather-like touch against the seam of her jeans. Clara nipped Caleb's earlobe before pushing his head back up to hers. She caught his gaze with hers. He made no move to kiss her anywhere, instead he watched her golden gaze with his own as his fingers unbuttoned her jeans. A gasp escaped her as his hand dove inside her underwear. "We have to…" his fingers found her clit, "…stop…" Clara realised another moan he brushed it repeatedly getting harder each time.

"You just have to say so," Caleb whispered softly. Clara pulled his head closely, desperate for his drugging kiss but he resisted settling for watching her as he massaged her pussy. Clara bowed her head until her forehead rested against his chest. "More," she whispered to him.

Caleb's movement changed as fingers dove inside her. Clara could feel her hips moving at their own accord. He kept a slow torturous rhythm. "I need…" Clara moaned against his lips. Caleb slowly withdrew his hand from her causing her to groan at the loss. He moved away pulling off his top. That second of air between them seemed to bring reasoning back to Clara.

They were in the living room with the door wide open and Howard had just been in the room. This was a mistake. A stupid and emotional mistake. Her eyes watched him. But he could be worth a mistake, said a voice in her mind.

"You really should stop overthinking everything," Caleb said calling Clara to pay attention to him instead of her thoughts. She gazed up at him.

"The doors open," was all Clara could come up with. Caleb grinned down at her as he caged her in.

"Easily rectified," he stated before throwing her over his shoulder.

Clara squealed and clawed at his back as she tried to get free. He just laughed and carried her out of the room. Clara watched as the Pack stood in the kitchen watching them move through the house. Embarrassment filled her.

They reached Caleb's room and he dropped her on his bed. But Clara had gone beyond wanting nothing but him, instead she wanted to hit him for carrying her like a piece of meat. "You asshole!" she growled at him, "They all saw! What are they going to think now?!"

"What they think is their business?" he shrugged before crawling over her. She knew she wasn't in the position to fight whilst she was lying on her back.

"We can't do this, Caleb" she said leaning as far down as she could on the bed trying to put space between them.

"Okay," he said staying where he was over her, "why?"

"Because above everything else going on, we just had my murdering ex-boyfriend in the living room" Clara confessed knowing that it would cause the mood to change.

Caleb shot off her growling. "Why didn't you say something to me sooner?!"

"You better not be turning this back on me?!" she yelled at him, causing him to stop growling.

"No, I'm not," he stopped himself, "if I had known, I would have…" Clara smiled at him. She moved until she stood in front of him.

"How can you act like this after knowing me for only a couple of weeks?"

"Why can't I?" he asked.

"Because you don't know me," she smiled solemnly up at him.

"I know you're a fighter, a survivor, and the fact you secretly care for everyone here even if you don't admit it to yourself." He said catching her off-guard as he brushed his thumb against her lips, "For the past few days you've tried to help out where you can because you don't believe you deserve to live here."

She stared up at him. She shouldn't be here. She was so vulnerable to the man in front of her. He could see into her soul and with every day he learnt something new about her. Slowly Clara looked up to him, she watched as his smile faltered. She pressed her lips against his in a caste kiss. Caleb didn't let her pull away and break the spell.

Instead he picked her up and walked her over to the bed. "You're addictive," he said as he laid her down with a kiss. His hands moved to remove her top as they kissed. Clara clawed his back trying to pull him closer. She needed him. He was her drug. He moved away from their kiss moving further down, never moving completely away from her. Clara hurried helped him pulling her t-shirt and bra off. His lips encircled her bare nipple almost as soon as her breasts were on show causing her arch up into him with a moan. Her fingers fumbled with his jeans desperate to feel him completely naked against her.

The sound of the zipper soothed her as her hand slowly grazed the hair there. "In a hurry there?" he chuckled against her tit. She smiled at him before taking hold of him. Caleb's hands moved to relieve himself of his jeans. Clara pumped her hand up and down his member. He moaned and teased within her grasp. He nipped the side of her neck before pulling her hand away.

He ripped off her jeans causing her to gasp as she saw the grin on his face. "You're beautiful," he said smiling down at her. Clara blinked at him. He moved until he almost rested fully above her. His fingers traced every scar along her torso making her super aware of every battle she had ever been in, "So strong too" he smiled softly at her face. Clara wasn't used to this. Tenderness, kindness and going slow wasn't what she did. She never had. Howard had been rough and what they did was never loving, not really, it was just plain fucking. They kept too many secrets from each other to truly be loving partners.

Yet Caleb caressed every inch of her before moving to her core. By then she was soaking wet and aching for him. The moans that escaped her seemed like they belonged to another body. He licked, sucked and kissed her everywhere. As he entered her, Clara could feel herself clinging to him, completely accepting him. She needed him like she needed her next breath.

Her hands clawed and gripped his back urging him to go faster. Her lips kissed his jaw line as his kissed her neck. His hands moved to hold hers above her head. His face came into view. His golden eyes stared down at hers calling to her wolf. Yet her wolf was happy to sit back and enjoy. Caleb changed his paced going faster and faster causing her moans to grow louder. Her body moved to match his. Their lips brushed and their breath mingled. Her head rolled back and further as she reached her peak. A roaring groan filled the air.

CHAPTER 7

Clara's felt way too warm where she was. A heavy weight held her down on the bed. She moved her arms stroking the arm that curled around her waist anchoring her to the hard body behind her. She snuggled closer to the solid body cocooning her. Her eyes opened as she looked at the blank wall opposite her. Her logical mind slowly woke up reprimanding her about what had happened last night. Once they had started, they hadn't stopped, as if they had been starved of each other for years. Clara nibbled her bottom lip. It shouldn't have happened. Howard had been in the living room just minutes before they had pounced on each other.

Caleb had offered her what she had needed. He offered comfort and warmth that she had missed for years. It wasn't until last night that Clara had realised just what she had been doing for the past few years. She had used Howard to give her physical warmth and comfort but nothing more than that. She had kept her distance. Slowly Clara turned around facing the sleeping man next to her. There was one question that stayed in her mind echoing her fears; had she used him as well?

She brushed a hand against his cheek, letting her fingers follow the line of his jawline. The arm around her tightened but Caleb made no notion that he was waking up any time soon. Clara smiled as she took in his features. His low brow line was relaxed with sleep whereas he usually had a crease in the middle whenever they seemed to talk. Clara pulled her hand away and slowly pulled herself away from him. The arm that held her loosened its hold allowing her to climb out of his bed. The whole room scented like him; woody and wild. She sighed grabbing her clothes from the floor before escaping to the bathroom.

She climbed into the shower allowing the hot sprays of water to run down her body washing away any scent of Caleb. It felt wrong and that new part of her scolded her for the move. That part wanted everyone to know that she was with Caleb, that she was his. She shook her head, not truly understanding the animal part of her in this matter. She cleaned her hair and made sure every itch of her body was clean. Stepping out she could still smell him on her clothes and told herself that she wasn't wearing them again until they were clean as well. Growling to herself she wrapped herself in a towel and towel dried her hair before venturing out to her own room.

The room was still bare of any personalisation, but it was hers. It was a sanctuary she hadn't realised she had needed in her life until she came here. Slowly she dropped her clothes on a growing pile of laundry and headed over to her closet. She pulled out a pair of cut-off jeans and a baggy grey t-shirt before she tied her hair back. Confident she looked okay and not like someone who had spent their night sleeping with someone else, she wandered downstairs.

As she stepped into the living area eyes landed on her, noses sniffed the air until they were unsatisfied with the result they got. Her gut dropped as she met all of their gazes. They were expecting something else. They had expected us to be mated, said a moody voice in her head. Her eyes widened before she fled the room. She rushed into Caleb's study and cursed herself for doing so. Having spent her morning routine trying to get his scent off her and out of her head she had run to the comfort of it. Sighing she sat down in his desk chair and let herself relax slightly. She had been with the pack for almost three weeks now, her mind had settled into place although hearing her wolf speaking to her frightened her slightly. Clara shook her head and eyed the desk.

Curiosity killed the cat, but Clara was intrigued by the pile of files on the desk and the fact the computer was on and open pulled her in. She spared a glanced at the door before diving into the pile of files. She found hers and read through it. It was everything The Order had written up about her. Shock run through her. The packs could hack into The Order's systems and they probably didn't even know. According to them she was deceased. Her training records, ranking and even mission lists were all in the file. She sighed. Her whole life fitted into a folder no thicker than a brochure. She threw it done on the desk and started taping away at the computer.

At first, she curiously looked at all the files on the system before she found out how to access The Order's system. She wondered whether she could access it with her code, they should have wiped her from their system if she was dead. Unless. She typed her passcode and identity codes in. She grinned ear to ear as the software welcomed her. Clara did something she never did; she investigated her history. She searched through the background research they must have done on her. Pages flickered before her eyes. Her high school results, every name of the foster parents she had had. Then there it was. In pure black and white. Her parent's death. Tear sprung anew in her eyes. Laura and Jonathan Richards found dead after bridge gave way under the car, their daughter, however, was found safe on the bank of the river. Clara looked at the date. 31st March 1991. Instantly she opened the web browser and started searching something she hadn't looked up since she was a teenager.

Hours past and she never left the office. Clara knew everyone must have known where she was as she could hear them talking in the other room along. But she carried on printing anything she found intriguing or confusing. Something didn't make sense. She had delved even further into her parent's lives. They had been a normal couple; her mother had been a teacher at a local primary school whilst her dad worked as a mechanic. She investigated their families. Something was strange about her father's family. Alexandra Volkov a Russian woman who had fled with her family from Russia to England just after world war one. She had died at the age of forty-two during the blitz leaving her daughter Elizabeth behind. Elizabeth Hays had married when she was eighteen and had been pregnant at the time. But she had died young after her husband left her leaving Alyssa's father, Jonathan alone. Alyssa gnawed of her lip. This was getting confusing.

Returning to The Order's database she typed in family members names. Nothing came up until she typed in 'Alexandra Volkov'. Clara's eyes widened. She pressed print and turned off the computer. She turned and faced the pile that had printed out for her about her great-grandmother. She picked it up and got comfortable in her seat. Flipping it over she stared at the photo of the woman. She had been beautiful with what Clara could tell from the black and white photo. The word 'DECEASED' was stamped at the bottom of the photo. Clara carefully put the photo face up on the desk before reading up on her Great-grandmother.

It was as clear as day what was written in the file and it pulled the rug out from under Clara. Her mind did somersaults as she tried to work out how she had gotten so far from her roots. Tears filled her eyes. "Shit!" she yelled before slamming the papers onto the desk. She rushed out of the house stripping as she went. Her body was a step ahead of her. As soon as she was free of her clothes, her body morphed in to her blond wolf form. She howled sorrowfully into the sky before charging off into the woodlands to take her anger out on whoever she came across.

***

Caleb and Michael charged out of the living room as soon as they heard her swear and slam something down. They caught a glimpse of her shifting. Caleb had shoved Michael away as her naked form had come into view even from a brief moment. But it was the howl that gained their attention. Michael dove after her as Caleb walked into his study. Paper had fallen on the floor. He moved to pick it up, he spotted the name and quickly scanned the pages as he picked them up. Confused he looked towards the other piles of paper that Clara had gathered up. Shock threw him.

She wasn't just any bitten stray. Caleb looked out of the window to see Michael backing up towards the house. Caleb rushed to him. "She's in a full-blown rage" Michael said as he limped back indoors, "We're better off waiting for her to return on her own once she's given the strays out there a run for their money".

"Michael can you organise the mess in the office for me?" he sighed before shifting and going after Alyssa.

He charged through the woodland following her scent. He stopped as he caught hold of Michael's scent and the faint taste of blood on the wind. She had given his beta a warning blow and he had backed down. Growling low Caleb started off again searching for his female. He dove through the bushes hoping to find her along their side of the territory lines, but in his gut, he knew she had gone over. Swallowing his pride, he jumped over the line and charged off following her scent.

He had been running for two miles before he found her attacking strays. Most of the group that had been waiting outside his territory for a glimpse at the female had already backed away to lick their wounds. Yet the she-wolf wasn't letting up she snapped, growled and slashed at the lone wolves. She ached for blood. Caleb howled gaining her attention. She turned on him growling. He tilted his head and slowly rounded her back into the woodlands. She snapped at him the whole time back she backed up. The blond she-wolf allowed herself to be rounded up back onto the territory lines. Once there she pounced. Her teeth dug into his back whilst Caleb just shook her off and pinned her down. She wriggled and snapped but never tried to do any real damage. After a few minutes she relaxed and whimpered. As she surrendered, Clara's body eased itself bank into human form.

"Why the hell did you come after me?!" she yelled as soon as he shifted.

"You can't go off on your own," Caleb answered calmly, knowing why she was emotional.

"You don't have to keep saving me, I can look after myself" she yelled.

"I know you can," once Caleb answered calmly.

"Then why do you keep doing it?!" she shouted her plea.

"Because you're one of us, you deserve protection as much as the next person"

"No, I don't. I'm a murderer. I shot my people in cold blood all out of damn ignorance!" she yelled, "I have no right to be saved!"

She moved to storm off away from the territory, away from safety in order to put herself in danger. "Will you calm down!" he yelled after her, causing her back to go straight as her anger turned back round on to him.

"Maybe you didn't hear me. I have killed our kind. I probably killed a few of your family members. Your pack knows it. I know it. Hell, I've probably had a hand in killing my own…" she stopped tears fell from her eyes. Caleb stepped towards her hoping to comfort her back she straightened up and pushed the tears back. "You have no right to tell me to calm down. You have no right to save me."

"You listen to me," he growled, "I have every right. As your alpha I command you to return to the house!" He hated himself for ordering her about a way he had never done to any of his pack. Her eyes widened as she followed his command. It was one thing an alpha could do that, any command they made their pack members would follow. Many chose not to follow through, some never issued a command in their lifetime. They merely asked and assumed it would get done. They would not lead by force.

Caleb's gut retched as he watched her go into her house. Her body moving on its own as her wolf took command of her human body. He followed her and pulled her into his study. "I saw all of this before I came to get you." He said pointing at the now ordered papers. Her eyes stayed downcast as he spoke. "It's not your fault. You didn't know, but they did".

Her head shot up, "They must have known" he repeated to her causing her eyes to widen. He stepped closer to her, "They are to blame, not you".

"How can you say that?" she cried, "Why would they have recruited me if they had known of my connections? They hate us!"

"We will find out. I promise" he said stepping towards her. Clara shot away from him keeping her distance. Her eyes watched him closely.

As Clara stared up at Caleb, she couldn't believe him. She couldn't understand why he wanted her to stay so much. He had seen everything she had found. He knew that she had worked with The Order an agency she now knew had hunted her grandmother. How was he still standing in front of her with sympathy etched clearly on his handsome features? He reached out for her, but Clara backed away again. He confused her. She couldn't understand why he had saved her to begin with, why he worked so hard to make her stay, or why he was still here before her. She had been with the pack for less than three weeks. Yes, they had slept together but he shouldn't feel committed to her. He reached out again catching her wrist before she could evade him.

"Just stop!" she shouted at him. His eyes widened as he released her. "How can you be so understanding about all of this? First you save me then you house me and look after me, and now you're protecting me and…. just…Just why?!"

Caleb stayed quiet. He knew why but he didn't want to scare her away. She was his mate and the information in the pile of papers didn't change that. He honestly didn't care what she had done. Instead he was angry at The Order. Once he got Clara to calm down and go set her mind on something else he would read in greater depth, but he was already sure that The Order were to blame as to why she never knew her family.

Clara waited for an answer that never came. She watched his face for any hint of expression as to why. Anxiety took over as she hoped for any answer to come from him. Whether she hoped it was because she was the only She-wolf in existence or the fact he had in some why he had come to care for her, she didn't know but at least she would be wanted in some regard. She stepped further away, her eyes never leaving his face as he seemed to distantly gaze on her. After a few minutes of silence, her anxiety and impatience got the best of her.

"I think its best I leave," she muttered, "I'm only bringing you trouble". At that she left the room, her head hung low. The only thing that made her feel worse was that Caleb didn't reply or argue her instead he accepted it.

CHAPTER 8

When she had left the office, Clara had done what none of the pack had expected. Within minutes she was heading out of the front door with a rucksack on her back full of her clothes. She didn't say any goodbyes or even turned around to face anyone. Her eyes focused for a few minutes on the closed office where Caleb still hid behind, and then she left. Michael couldn't believe it. She had settled into their pack extremely well, and for the first time he had seen his Alpha have some fun rather than just going about his day helping others. They all waited for the office door to open and to see Caleb rush out to bring her back. But they waited in vain.

The next few days they watched as Caleb just paced the house in silence, his mind pondering everything. It was only when he spent the fifth day completely locked up in his office did Michael go in and question him.

"What is going on, Cal?" Michael asked as he knocked on the locked door.

"It's for the good of the Pack," Caleb replied solemnly.

"What is?"

"That she's left," Caleb murmured.

"Do you really believe that?" Michael asked trying the door handle. The door was still locked.

"I have to," Caleb replied.

"Open the door, Cal," Michael asked, "You can't think all these things through without talking to at least one of us".

"What is there to talk through? She's already left," Caleb replied harshly.

"It's not like we can't track her down," Michael said leaning against the door. He paused and listened to what was going on inside the office. He could hear Caleb pacing and huffing in the room. "Did you ever stop to think that maybe she didn't really want to leave?" he suggested. The office fell silent, "If you think about it, she was naturally an Alpha. If she saw herself as the alpha here, then she would have been thinking of the pack rather than herself when she chose to leave. Just like you are when you're processing her decision".

The door opened and Michael finally got a glimpse of Caleb. He looked exhausted and haggard. He was still wearing the same clothes as the day Clara left.

"Do you think she left for that reason?" Caleb asked as he peered around the door.

"We won't know until we go find her," Michael smiled. He expected Caleb to grin back, to be eager to hunt down his female. But the Caleb that stood before him just sighed and shook his head.

"We can't go get her," he said, "If The Order haven't found her yet, they'll follow us if we leave to go get her".

"Decoy?" Michael suggested.

"We have no idea who they'd accept to follow".

"I think it's time to recruit some Strays," Michael grinned.

***

Clara sat on a cold metal dinner chair in a motel room staring out of the window. Her eyes focused on the small metal door on what looked like a small warehouse. Only those from The Order knew that it wasn't a warehouse. Behind that door was one entrance into the main headquarters. She had already watched hunters coming and going for the past three days. No one had noticed that there was a Lycan staying opposite an entrance. She figured no Lycan in their right mind would even walk within a mile radius of a place that reeked of death. And that thought fitted right into her plan.

Her eyes narrowed as the door opened. There he was. Howard. He stepped out looking at his phone. A group of five hunters followed and stood there. All of them were dressed in black from head to toe, guns rested in their holsters on their hips. Taking a deep breath, Clara left her seat. Dress in casual clothes that were bright enough to make her stand out, she walked over to the bed. She picked up the gun she was swiped from a hunter four days ago. He hadn't recognised her when she had creeped up on him. It was one swift twist of the neck and he went down. Clara quietly and quickly checked that the mag was fully loaded before readying it for her mission. The wolf inside growled at the thought of using a gun rather than its teeth and claws, but it understood why it had to be done.

She closed her eyes for a moment and pictured the pack in her mind. She missed them. Her wolf begged to go back, to run with them, and to stay by

Caleb's side. Clara told herself she couldn't go back, not until she could rectify what she had done as a hunter. She had no right to life with other Lycan's until she avenged her family. Growling at the thought that her family had died at the hand of The Order, she headed out of the door. Once down the hallway, Clara stepped out of the front of the motel and stared at the group. They were moving towards two standard black SUVs as she stepped out. With a grim firm line of a smile Clara raised her gun. This time she had to lead on a wild goose chase, before taking her revenge.

Her finger pulled on the trigger twice. The right front wheels of both SUVs blew causing the whole group to pause and look around. She pulled on the trigger again, the front passenger window shattered. She huffed. The Order never thought to make their cars bulletproof, in their ethos no Lycan would ever use a gun. The hunters moved around the SUV their eyes intent on her. Howard stood stock still where he was. She blew a kiss before sending on more shoot, this one clipped his ear.

In a blink she moved. Clara had her path set out in her mind as she ran. She darted right down one alley leading the hunters away from the entrance. Once they turned the corner after her, she darted left towards a public car park. She slid across the gravel and under a blue Land Rover. From under there she shimmied out of her clothes, keeping her eyes on the opening to the car park. Once naked she quickly slipped the gun under her clothes before shifting. Her wolf was more than happy to come forwards. It was time to fight with claws and fangs. Keeping down and out of view, Clara watched as the Hunter's scouted the area.

Two hunters headed down a path to the left of the car park, while the other three headed down the road to the right. Once they were out of the view, Clara focused on the only person that stayed patrolling the car park, Howard. He slowly stalked the car park, peering into each parked car as he went. Only a small voice in Clara's mind told her to run, but instead she waited. Howard got two cars away before Clara pouched.

They landed on the rough gravel ground sending stones flying. Clara stayed silent as she cuffed his neck with her fangs. Her front paws pinned his forearms, stopping Howard from reaching his gun. A low thunderous rumble slowly grew from her chest. The human part of her was hesitant to act and rip out his throat, yet the wolf part wanted him gone.

"Clara, I won't hurt you," Howard said softly, "You still mean a lot to me. I'm sorry I left you". Clara lifted her head and stared down at him. He still looked the same, and his expression was sincere. "You need to run, The Order won't rest now they know you exist," he whispered. Her eyes widened. Why was he telling her this?

"If you head back to the Ash Pack, The Order will order a kill mission on the whole pack," he warned. Clara's heart dropped. She wanted so much to head back to Caleb and his pack, but the idea of them dying was enough to make her plan never to return. "You need to head North," he ordered, "Once you get to Birmingham, you need to find Harley Finn. He'll help you escape The Order".

Slowly Clara backed off Howard and stood there staring at him in shock. He sat up and did a quick survey of the area before leaning towards her.

"I mean it when I say I'm sorry," He said, "You need to run now before…"

Bang.

Clara fell to the ground, pain radiated in her right hind leg. A howl escaped her. She had stayed still too long in an open area. Hurt she looked towards Howard who had jumped up with his back to her.

"Good job, Jones," said a very familiar voice, General McKenzie. Her gut instantly dropped. "I never thought we might bring her back alive". The old man sounded smug. Slowly Clara pulled herself up and stepped closer to Howard. Her golden eyes focused on the general and the young hunter next to him. His granddaughter, Natalie. Clara wanted to destroy that skinny ambitious hunter.

"I told you, he would keep her distracted," Natalie smirked. Clara stilled; her head raised to look up at

Howard. Unable to see his face she tried not to believe that he had just acted like he wanted to help her.

"Put a chain on her and drag her back," order the General. Clara limped backwards. With wide eyes she watched the humans around her.

Howard turned around holding a silver chain firmly in his hands. His whole demeanour told her that he was going to follow the order. Fear ran through her as she whimpered and looked up at his face. She expected to see a cold expression, with no emotions. But instead there was sadness there. There she saw her answer. He mouthed one word.

Run.

Clara didn't wait. She dived back from the Land Rover as Howard spun round to the General. Gunfire sounded behind as she shifted back. She tried to shove on her clothes. Just as she got her top and pants on a hand pulled her out by the ankle. With quick thinking she grabbed the gun and got ready to fire. As her head appeared from under the Land

Rover, she pulled the trigger and shot the Hunter that had dragged her out from under the car in the face. Jumping up to her feet, she walked round the car shooting at every hunter she caught in her sight. When her eyes landed on the General, she spied Howard on the ground bleeding. Her heart sunk.

"I should have expected you to change," General McKenzie said, "Your relative had the same conviction to stay alive. But then she met me" he smiled coldly. He raised his gun. But his age, and time in the office rather on the field had slowed him down. Clara shot at him without aiming anywhere vital, as she rushed to Howard's side. Natalie jumped forwards trying to block Clara from getting to Howard.

With no care, Clara slammed her fist home breaking Natalie's nose and knocking her out cold. The General just looked in disgust at his granddaughter, before looking at Clara. A Gun fired in the distance and Clara screamed out.

"You were always emotional," the General tutted, "It was your biggest downfall".

"No it wasn't," Clara growled as her fangs descended, "It will be yours". In a blink she shifted and launched herself at the General. Guns fired trying to catch her with bullets as she jumped back and forth at the General. Each time she delivered sharp deep bites to the old man. She backed off as the General fell to the floor, she sniffed the air and the smell of death was creeping in.

That smell called her to look at Howard. His face was pale. She let out a howl in remorse. For the first time, her call was answered.

Clara stilled and sniffed the air. The Pack. They were here. Her heart jumped in her chest. She couldn't see them, but they were nearby. She had heard them. Another shot fired. She yelled out. Clara fell to the ground shaking. Her whole body felt cold. She watched in horror as her wolfen body was forced back into her human form.

"You are such a stupid bitch!" hissed Natalie, who held her grandfather's gun. "You were meant to die on that mission!"

"What…" Clara coughed out.

"The Order was done with you!" Natalie yelled marching closer to Clara's shaking naked form. "Now I'm going to finish the job".

Clara closed her eyes waiting for the shot to come.

A rumbling growl sounded ahead of Clara. Peaking through her lashes she spied a collection of eight large male wolves. Natalie had turned around trying to work out who to aim at. Clara tried to push herself up off the floor a noticed that the other Hunters in the area were all on the ground with various types of injuries. While Natalie was distracted, Clara tried to shift back to wolf form. Her body wasn't listening. Instead the only parts that appeared were her fangs and claws.

Caleb's black wolf launched himself at Natalie while the others circled around.

"Come closer and I shoot her!" Yelled Natalie. That threat caused Caleb to stop. He growled as Natalie pointed the gun at Clara.

"You were never hunter material," Clara said catching Natalie's attention, "Did you hope to walk in granddaddy's footsteps? Were you going to be the golden child?"

"You bitch!" Natalie yelled and fired. Clara fell back, pain scorched her upper body. Her claws dug into something soft, as the taste of blood slipped into her mouth.

With a roaring growl the wolves around her pouched on the slim hunter. Clara ignored the fighting and tried to get back up. Her body felt weak. She eyes her hands, that had dug into Howards leg when she was shot. Her eyes landed on a small cut just small distance away from the claw marks. Clara quickly checked herself. She could taste blood, but it wasn't hers.

"Shit," Clara murmured as she leaned closer into Howard and sniffed. The smell of death around him was fading, even though it lingered in the air from the other bodies around.

"Are you okay?" asked a voice, Clara felt in tune to. She looked up to see a naked Caleb kneeling by her.

"Fine, but I …" Clara answered,

"I can smell it," Caleb replied, "But are you okay?" He asked again.

"I'm okay," She gave a weak smile. Caleb brushed his fingers over her shoulder where she had been shot, before he leaned closer.

"Let's go home," he whispered to her before planting a kiss on her shoulder. Clara closed her eyes and relished the moment. Caleb scent surrounded her.

"We can't leave him," she replied.

"And we won't," Michael added in, catching her attention. Clara looked up to see all of the pack surrounding them.

"Come on, time to get you back home," added in Edmund with a smile. For the first time, Clara didn't feel afraid of the man.

CHAPTER 9

Caleb stood at the base of the medical bed where he's newest pack member lay unconscious. The small nick of Clara's fang had been enough to change him. Caleb hadn't tried to convince Clara to accept their mating bond, not when she had just changed her ex-boyfriend. Part of him, wished that the guy she called Howard had caught the fever during the change and died. That way, Clara would be all his. But instead the hunter had taken to the bite just like every other man bitten by a Lycan. He knew he'd have to accept the male into his pack, or risk Clara possibly leaving to follow him. Caleb sighed. He knew the bond was there between him and Clara's wolves but how was he going to convince Clara to choose him when the man she had loved before was now the same species as herself.

Begrudgingly he left the basement and headed outside to the back garden. No one was out there expecting her. Clara turned her head and looked back at him from where she sat on the grass. Her smile met her eyes. Caleb couldn't help but smile back, even though his mind was fixed on the fact she may not choose him.

"Come here," Clara called. She patted the ground next to her when he didn't move. Still Caleb stayed where he was just watching her. He didn't want to get to close, in case it would just end up being memories. He watched as Clara stood up, brushed herself off and headed over to him.

His wolf begged him to meet her half way, but the human side wanted to back away. He wasn't ready for a heart break. Clara marched over to him and didn't stop until they were toe to toe.

"You've been avoiding me all week since we got back," She said softly as she reached out to hold on to his hands with hers.

"I've just been busy sorting out loose ends," He mumbled his reply.

"It has nothing to do with Howard?" She queried looking him dead in the eye. Their he saw the challenge. She wanted him to admit something. Her eyes shone golden trying to call to his wolf.

"No," He lied. His gut hurt as he did so.

"I think it does," Clara said sharply, "You haven't touched me since he's scent changed to Lycan".

"Clara…" Caleb started.

"You really think he's more important now? Now you have a new wolf, that's it." She butted in.

"Clara…"

"You really take your role as Alpha way too seriously. It's all work with you. What now you have to housetrain the new puppy yourself? Get someone else to do it." She pushed.

"What? So, you can train him yourself?" Caleb said harshly, "Are you wanting lover boy all to yourself now he's tried to save you?"

"You idiot!" Clara shouted.

"You must have a damsel in distress disorder. Any man saves you and they have your attention," Caleb added.

"Will you shut up!" Clara roared at him. Caleb paused and looked closely at Clara. "I'm wanting time with you, you idiot!"

"With me?" he queried.

Clara sighed and lifted her hands to his cheeks. She stroked the slight five o'clock shadow along his jaw. "I've missed you," she said softly, "All I wanted when I was gone was to come back here and curl up with you. I know it doesn't make any sense, but you feel like the other half of me. When you're not around, I feel lost".

Caleb didn't need to hear anymore. He grabbed her by the waste and pulled her in closer. His mouth devoured hers. Her hands moved around as her fingers moved into his hair. She kept her kiss on hers as his hands lowered to ass. He squeezed her firm cheeks and pushed her mound against his hardness. Neither of them cared that they were outside. With quick fingers, Caleb moved her hand around to the front of her jeans and dove in to find her already wet. A contented rumble hummed from his chest as he pushed his finger into her. He captured her moan in his mouth as his tongue danced with hers. Clara's fingers tightened their grip on his hair.

Within seconds he had her writhing on his hand, her moans become louder and more breathless.

"I want you," She moaned as she lowered her hands to his jeans to try and free him. Caleb removed his hand of her and quickly shredded his jeans with claws.

"I need you," he replied with a rough rumbling voice. His mouth descended back onto hers. Clara took over and pushed them back up against the wall of the house. Pulling back from her, Caleb grinned, and he twisted them round so her back was against the wall. Her cheeks were flushed, and her lips were swollen. His mind instantly wondered what her other lips tasted like. In a blink he pulled her jeans down to her ankles taking her thong with them and went down on his knees.

"What are you…" A gasp escaped her as Caleb kissed her bald mound. With a quick dart of a tongue, he licked along the seem before parting the lips. He kissed her clit, before sucking hard of the swollen orb. Clara's hands instantly moved to hold on to his head as her eyes fluttered closed. Lightening shocks filled her body as his tongue flicked her nub as he sucked on it.

"Fuck," was all she could say in the moment before he put his finger back inside her. Warmth flooded her body as her hips moved at their own accord. Caleb kept a firm hold on her hips with one hand as he ate out her pussy as if he had been starving for years. Clara could feel her orgasm building and building, but she didn't want to cum on his tongue. She had missed his touch so much. She wanted him inside her. She needed him inside her.

With a sharp pull on his hair she pulled his mouth away from her. He growled up at her, his eyes golden. Her wolf inside practically panted at the sight, while her pussy got even wetter. With a smile and a growl, she pulled him up until he once again towered over her.

"Mine," she growled at him as she moved one hand to massage his proud member. Her growled in returned as he lips met hers. Clara could taste herself on his tongue and her body felt like it was on fire. She pulled him as close as she could and lifted one leg up around her hips. Caleb grinned against her kiss as he gripped her ass. Positioning himself quickly he hammered into her. Clara gasped and moaned with every thrust. Her hands clawed at his back, causing the scent of blood to mix in with the scent of their lovemaking.

Caleb slowly kissed her neck as he thrusted, while Clara rested her forehead against his shoulder. Quickly he lifted her other leg and pushed her right against the wall until it was just him and the wall taking her weight.

"Mine," he groaned as his thrusts quickened, "You're mine".

"All yours," she moaned in reply as her mouth kissed his neck.

The beast pushed forwards in her mind as his claws dug into her ass as he thrusted. Their scent mixed as they fucked harder and harder. Her body shook and shivered as orgasms rolled on straight after another. Her mouth burned as her fangs descended. Without thinking she bit down hard on Caleb's shoulder as her body trembled with another orgasm. A howl filled her ears before a sharp but blissful pain hit her own shoulder. Her orgasm reached a new height as fireworks took over her vision.

They collapsed to the ground panting. Caleb took Clara's weight and sat with her in his lap. Clara rested her head on his shoulder and sighed while his hands stroked her back. Everything felt right. Leaning back, she gazed at his face. Her human side told her it was still too soon to say what her wolf wanted to howl for the whole world to hear. But the man that held her felt like home, the home she had been waiting to find since she lost her parents.

"I love you," Caleb said surprising her. His warm brown eyes watched hers as she stayed silent. Panic had set into his stare when she didn't reply straight away.

"I love you too," Clara smiled after a couple of minutes of watching him. With a soft caress she stroked his jawline, "You are everything I need," she added planting a kiss on his lips.

Within seconds their kiss deepened again. Their hands roamed each other's bodies as their passion set alight again.

A rough cough caused them to stop.

"Can you put each other down for a moment?" said Michael from the kitchen, "The newbie is awake asking for Clara". A growl escaped Caleb. No other male was every going to have her. Clara chuckled, kissed him on the cheek before getting off of his lap.

"Maybe next time, we continue this is bed with a locked door," she whispered to him. Clara grabbed her jeans from the ground and slipped them on, not bothering to put her thong back on. A feral part of Caleb was glad that she was going commando, his scent would be surrounding her when she went to meet the new wolf. Her ex would know exactly who she belonged to now. He watched as she walked into the house.

"You might want to follow her, he has some interesting facts about The Order," Michael said coming out of the kitchen to lean against the backdoor frame.

"I'll give it a few minutes," Caleb said with a grin. His wolf wanted to relish in the memory of finally claiming his mate.

"If you're going to stay there, at least put your pants back on," Michael huffed before casting his glance to the garden, "He thinks there may be more females out there".

Clara stepped into the medical room to see Howard sitting up on his bed cot. Only a month ago, she would have felt glad to be alone in a room with him. She would have pulled him back into bed with her. But now her nose wrinkled at his scent, it didn't feel right.

"I meant it when I said sorry," he said, "I should have let you run, or helped you to get out of The Order. If I did, then none of this would have happened".

"We can't change the past," Clara replied sitting on the bed opposite him, "If you had helped me, I may have never found a pack that accepted me even with my past as a hunter". She wanted to add that she would have never met Caleb, but she'd wait to deliver that news.

"The Order needs to be stopped," Howard lifted his head to look her dead in the eye.

"I think every shifter in the world would agree with you," Clara replied.

"No, I mean it," Howard pushed, "I was doing research when I found out that you were the female Lycan".

"What did you find out?" Caleb said as he walked into the medical room with Michael. He didn't stop walking until he was sitting next Clara. When his body touched hers a part of him that he didn't realise was tense calmed down. Instinctively her hand moved to rest on his knee. His wolf was content enough to pay attention to what Howard was about to say.

"Clara isn't the first hunter to be changed during a hunt," Howard said, "and she isn't the first female".

"If there were others we'd know about it," Michael scoffed in disbelief.

"There's an ex-hunter living just outside of Birmingham in Cannock Chase, he's been helping the bitten hunters go into hiding," Howard said.

"Yeh, and what's this man's name?" Michael said. He wasn't believing it at all. For fifty years, males have had to either settle down with human women without knowing whether they were their true mates or go it alone. If there were females out there, he was sure more Lycans would be talking about it. He knew strays often talked about trying to hunt down females, the mythical ones that a friend of a friend had spotted. But they were nothing but myths now.

"His name is Harley Finn," Howard replied, "I don't know how many females he's helped. But there's a reason why The Order recruits the people it does"

"What's that reason?" Caleb asked.

"We all have shifter Heritage," Howard replied.

"We all do?" Clara quizzed.

"It's why we can match the strength of shifters," Howard almost spat, "They may train us, but they recruit us by researching our family trees. That's why they need to be stopped".

"Why would they recruit us to kill our own kind?" Clara queried.

"General McKenzie, was known as the Exterminator in his day," Howard said, "He pushed for females to be killed, but when half-breeds were being born, he ordered the organization to keep track of them in case they changed."

"How do we stop them?" Caleb asked the group.

"We need to find the females first," Michael said, "They aren't safe in hiding, sooner or later someone is going to find them".

"Then that's what we will do," Clara said, "They need a safe haven, and we are going to need an army to take down The Order".

The group nodded with the idea. It was time for get ready for battle.

42942030R00103

Printed in Poland
by Amazon Fulfillment
Poland Sp. z o.o., Wrocław